We Are Made Of Diamond Stuff

We Are Made Of Diamond Stuff

Isabel Waidner

Dostoyevsky Wannabe Originals

An Imprint of Dostoyevsky Wannabe

First Published in 2019
by Dostoyevsky Wannabe Originals
All rights reserved
© Isabel Waidner

Dostoyevsky Wannabe Originals is an imprint of Dostoyevsky
Wannabe publishing.

Cover art by Linda Stupart
Cover design by Dostoyevsky Wannabe
www.dostoyevskywannabe.com
ISBN-978-1-9999245-3-9

Also by Isabel Waidner

Gaudy Bauble

*Liberating the Canon: An Anthology of Innovative
Literature*

"Isabel Waidner will save the nation & save our souls."

—Joanna Walsh

"*We Are Made Of Diamond Stuff* evokes a topsy-turvy, highly animated world to explore a declining empire's hopelessly fucked up inequities of class, race, queerness, and immigration status. At one point the narrator (who looks like Eleven from *Stranger Things* but who happens to be 36) blurts out, "Where's reality, I want to change it." This is one of the saddest lines I've ever read, perfectly rearticulating the "no there there" anxiety that Gertrude Stein attributed to modern life a century ago. In a world in which everything is stacked against them, Isabel Waidner's resourceful characters survive, not just physically but spiritually as well. Despite their unflinching vision into virulent social practices, they never lose heart."

—Dodie Bellamy

A list of referenced material can be found at the back of the book.

Contents

WAR CRYBABIES

I look like Eleven from *Stranger Things*, I'm 36. Similar hair, similar face. Similar fears (childhood terrors). I will not grow out my hair at the next opportunity (Season 2). Hello? Where am I. I'm alone on a beach. (What beach.) It's early. It's cold, where's my blue worker's jacket. It's raining lightly. (A British beach.) HELLO—!? Where is everyone. Oh good—it's getting lighter over the Solent (the stretch of water that separates the Isle of Wight from the British mainland). (This is the Isle of Wight off the south coast of England, the beach outside Ryde.) One, two, three Victorian military forts in the Solent—an early indication they have a thing about foreign invasion down here. Other than that, the beach is reassuringly pretty. Pinks and whites in this situation. Ochres. I take in the sea air—aaah. So far so good. But looking at the sea won't help. I have talents, I'll use them.

A soldier, look! The soldier is wearing an army green t-shirt with black polar bears on it, what does it mean. Black oversize joggers, white Reebok classic trainers. The pronoun is 'they', the soldier signals to include the black polar bears the white reeboks. Ok, I say. Like me, Shae (the soldier), the polar bears and the reeboks are new to the Isle of Wight. They are second generation economic migrants (Shae), ecological refugees (the polar bears) and African elopers I mean antelopes (the reeboks) from North West London. They are mobilising to storm a fort in the Solent for military training purposes. Come? Shae asks. Yes, I reply, wholeheartedly. My phone rings. Hello? According to the Fraud Detection Team, someone (not me) attempted to pay £85 to Poker Stars, then £500 to Paddy Power (betting sites), using my debit card. The Fraud Detection Team cancel my debit card with me on the beach. By the time I get off the phone, the moment to storm the fort has passed, we abort.

The Isle of Wight is home to a large working-class demographic. Shae, for one, works in a hotel in Ryde. Minimum wage rates, Shae says, but free board and lodging. Not bad, as far as it goes. I have no money, no debit card, I interview for a job. This is the manager—House Mother Normal, formerly of B. S. Johnson's eponymous novel (1971), pertaining to British avant-garde literature. House Mother Normal eyes me up, she looks unconvinced. Permission to work in the UK? she asks. Yes (EU national). Ability to communicate effectively in English? So so. Work experience? Twenty years of it (I have worked in all areas of the British hospitality and retail sectors). Kitchen? Yes (dying inside). When can you start? Yesterday.

A Styrofoam box containing raw squid and inky ice arrives for the kitchen. I get to it, I purge entire beaches and tiny digestive tracts from maritime bodies. Sand and intestines accumulate in the waste bucket, I'm building a private beach gutting squid. What if this were my beach (sandy refuse collecting in a bucket). What if this were my storm (my fort in the Solent)? I drop a cocktail umbrella into the bucket—it's like a beach parasol, only it lies on its side.

Freak weather events are fairly common on the Isle of Wight. Incidentally, the sea is YELLOW (yellow for volatile). I'm not going in this, I say. The polar bears survey the coastline for a while, the reeboks get halfway to the fort before they abort. Let's regroup tomorrow, Shae says.

The polar bears are novelists (infantry soldiers), the reeboks are poets (intelligence operatives). Given how busy Shae and I are, toiling, that's a beautiful thing. When they're not pursuing their aspirations (writing), the novelists and poets like to gnaw on raw squid. I deposit a saucerful under the kitchen sink. No one will notice—. GOOD MORNING! It's House Mother Normal patrolling her kitchen. I employ my foot to push the saucer of squid further under the kitchen sink where the polar bears and the reeboks are hiding with bated breath. Cut triangles that's it, House Mother Normal says. Nice and even. Then the arms, or is it tentacles—eugh. Pieces like Hula skirts. Hah! Hah! Put one round your finger, like this. Crikey—a lot of 'waste' in your bucket. Can you make soup. Don't bother rinsing—just boil the lot, the sand will sink to the bottom of its own accord. About your contract—, House Mother Normal says. Yes? I'm all ears. We'll keep it under the tax threshold, shall we. No National Insurance contributions, no sick pay, no holidays. Ok, I say. (Not ok.)

The original, B. S. Johnson's, House Mother Normal is in charge of a fictional nursing home. She has sidelines on the go, like watering down Vodka ('Boaka'), or altering the labelling of Penicillin bottles, for underhand profit. She exploits and abuses those in her care. *I want you to pour about a quarter of these bottles into one of the empty ones here until it's three-quarters full,* she says to an elderly resident at one point. *Three bottles pour a quarter out of, that is, until this one's also three-quarters full, and when you've got them all three-quarters full then top them up with water from your tap.* The recreational activities she provides are, if anything, worse. There's the Pass the Parcel game (roll the dice when a six comes up put on a hat and oven gloves quick as you can and hack away at the parcel until you either attain the gift of chocolate inside or someone else throws a six, whatever comes first). Turns out, there's no chocolate inside this parcel, only dog shit. Violent character, is B. S. Johnson's House Mother Normal. But B. S. Johnson violates House Mother Normal in turn, putting her through a public masturbation I mean bestiality scene—with dog, Ralphie—not once, not twice, but nine times over the course of the novel. Ghastly, really, but funny. Funny's important. It was a different time—. (Some BS there, B. S.?)

Funnily enough, this is now. This isn't a nursing home in '70s London, this is a no-star hotel—the 'New House of Normal'—in present-day Ryde. Like B. S. Johnson's, our House Mother Normal is a bully and exploiter—but if she has the original's entrepreneurial flair and resourcefulness, then so do we. (We have talents, we'll use them.) And who knows who's got what sexual kinks—no one knows, least of all me. I'm only new.

House Mother Normal puts her head round the door. No hot water. No whaaat—? Boiler gone, this is England. Boil the kettle to wash up or the grease will stick. Ok, I say, I get to it.

At a later point, House Mother Normal walks in on the polar bears FEEDING, the reeboks in a FRENZY. Who fed them? House Mother Normal works herself up over the polar bears and the reeboks freeloading. She is exploring the possibility of them fixing the boiler in exchange for their squid—. No! I say. The polar bears are novelists, the reeboks are poets, it is not within their remit nor skill set to fix an English boiler! In this case, House Mother Normal bans them from the kitchen for life. That'll come off *your* wages Mister, she says, I mean Miss—. Ok, I say. (Not ok.)

House Mother Normal is off. Off where? (Just off.) (Busy.) Now it's just Shae and I holding the fort—*this* fort, we're tied to *this* fort. (No storming the actual fort in the Solent, no dreaming of beaches, I put the cocktail umbrellas away.) It's nonstop from here—cleaning the bedrooms and communal areas, kitchen prep, washing up. Later, much later, Shae has a go at fixing the boiler. I'm still washing up, boiling the kettle until it, too, gives up the ghost.

Today is a different day. Shae's sweater features, most prominently, a lypard (a leopard). Also, fighter planes, rockets, explosions. Shrapnel and ★B★U★L★L★E★T★ ★R★A★I★N★. We are pacifists, but we have tanks on our sweaters. (The times we live in.) We gather at the beach like storm clouds—but the critical natural event is that the tide is so low WE CAN WALK TO THE FORT NO NEED FOR SEA LEGS. Attack! we issue our war cry. Onto the mudflats—! The white reeboks are mincemeat in a flash (the lypard, and also the mud). The rest of us are on target, we are in fact unstoppable—.

But what about peace, yes exactly. (The lypard has a massive tear in its eye, the lypard has a crazy smile on its face.) We get to the fort. We're about to enter—. A sign says Stay Out Stay Alive. (Does it—.) (It does.) We have second thoughts. (We really are war crybabies.) Attack? Shae whispers, but the lypard is already charging.

The lypard is ranging the foyer at night (a sinister presence, a danger). It has a massive tear in its eye, it tears through the foyer.

Chinooks are flying over the building at low altitude. Six or seven of the things (military helicopters). Is Britain at war? Warring agenda, Shae says. Sprawling back from the road, the New House of Normal is a three storey 1930s Art Deco block covered in scaffolding. A cylindrical structure (a tower) rises above the main entrance of the otherwise rectangular building (the 'block'). Three elongated Crittall windows run up the height of the tower (left, right and front-facing). Inside, the foyer is dark (the scaffolding). I'm wearing my brown hoodie with integrated gold necklace, ankle dusters and an overcoat. (It's overcoat weather indoors.) The reeboks are freaking out over the Chinooks. Why are they in our sky? Why, for that matter, are they called 'Chinooks'? Why does a British military helicopter carry the name of, of all things, the Chinook people?

It is US policy to name army aircrafts after Native American tribes or chiefs (the Boeing-Sikorsky Comanche, the Lockheed AH-56 Cheyenne). (The Bell OH-58 Kiowa.) Once, there was even a competition inviting the American public to 'NAME THAT BIRD'—'that bird' referring to a picture of an angry horsefly, sorry, the Sikorsky UH-60A four-bladed utility helicopter. Black Hawk was the winning entry, and also a Sauk leader, healer and warrior (1767-1838).

Is it a bird? Or is it a horsefly?

The policy was made official by authority of US Army Regulation 70-26, dated 4 April 1969: *All names are not acceptable. The name should appeal to the imagination, and should suggest an aggressive spirit and confidence in the capabilities of the aircraft. The name also should suggest mobility, agility, flexibility, firepower and endurance.*

Now, this isn't America, this isn't the Pacific Northwest. This is the Isle of Wight off the south coast of England, and 'Chinooks' everywhere! How can this be? Last September, the Ministry of Defence announced a five hundred million \$ deal to secure fourteen of the latest US-built Boeing CH-47 Chinook helicopters for the British Army (and that's on top of the rest), Shae says. I see, I say. Mutually beneficial trade relations—.

The reeboks are reading Tommy Pico the NDN (Native American) poet to process this sht on an individualised level at least. I can't write a nature poem, Pico writes in *Nature Poem* (2017), I wd slap a tree across the face. Slapping a tree across the face is rejecting white preconceptions that collude NDN people with nature. The same white preconceptions that collude NDN people with nature collude NDN people with a warring spirit. The stereotype extends into the expectation that, if y'r NDN, you shd suicide on yr reservation. You should die of crack cocaine or methamphetamine overconsumption—if y'r NDN, time ticks in funerals, Pico writes.

A stereotype is like a self-fulfilling prophecy maybe (in the popular sense of the term). You can't escape this reductive sht, this sht defines you.

The Reebok Working Class Plus, sorry, the Reebok

Workout Plus, is a classic trainer design connected to a particular British stereotype. (Not even funny, comparing the Msses Thing—the reeboks—to racial stereotyping.) (I'm not talking about the reeboks— I'm talking about Reebok classic trainers. Shae is wearing the things—.) Point being, you read NDN, just standing there. You read working-class, just wearing Reeboks (or not). Just talking. Just going about your life. At best, your resistance defines you: Pico writes *Nature Poem*. The reeboks are writing *Reebook*, their first full-length poetry collection. The polar bears are writing a novel (title tbc), and I'm filling in the 85-page application form for a document certifying permanent residence in the UK.

What's a British working-class stereotype, say it. No. Anything? No!

The gold necklace laced through the eyelets in my hoodie's collar could very easily make a weapon. How easily the imagination turns a thing like a necklace into a potential weapon. (The times we live in.) Anyone could hook a finger into my necklace and pull. Anyone could take my necklace, turn it into a slingshot and go at Shae. Anyone could self-harm or hang themselves using a necklace identical to my own. They use words as weapons, they use weapons as weapons, and sometimes both come together like in the Boeing CH-47 Chinook. The Germans, by the way, name their combat tanks after large cats (rather than after populations they colonised): *Jaguar*, *Puma 1*, *Puma 2*, *Weasel*, *Leopard 1*, *Leopard 2*. Oho! There's the lypard with its blond and brown pattern, its yellow eyes and its awful mouth—! (The mere mention of *Leopard 1*, *Leopard 2* attracts it.) The lypard is ranging the foyer in such a deranged manner, it's probably taking one of the reeboks right now. Let's have your necklace, Shae says, I'll put the pussycat on a leash. But horseflies are crowding the sky above Ryde, and Shae can't turn a necklace into a fly swat, can they.

POWDERED MILK

Relaxing in the foyer, I'm resting my plimsolls on the reception desk. I'm wearing my pink sweater with the green ribbons and rosettes arranged like a face. Eyes (o o), nose (v), mouth (_) and tears (| |) running past the hem of my sweater in the shape of green ribbons. You won something? Shae asks re the ribbons and the rosettes. It's my ribbon face sweater, it cost a bomb, I reply. I didn't win anything, I earned everything, including the right to put my feet on the reception desk here. Look at my face, I say, my face says nothing. Highly decorated, my ribbon face cries. It cries a ribbony river past the hem of my sweater, why's that.

I'm on Shae's tablet, putting my replacement debit card to good use (buying a cap to offset my ribbon face sweater—). But what's wrong, my payment won't go through. Won't it? Let's have a look, Shae says. It's not going through, they confirm. Your replacement debit card has no purchasing power.

Now there's a text from Barclays. I call the chargeable number. Another attempted fraud? No. No fraud. No funds on your account. No what? But Friday was payday! Zero, Barclays say. As a matter of fact, less than zero. Please contact your employer.

Shae checks their account, they haven't been paid either. They get on the phone to House Mother Normal. It's ringing (on loudspeaker). Where *is* Normal? I ask. (Still ringing.) We haven't seen her for weeks. Upstairs, Shae replies. Cutting drugs (black market PrEP, or crack cocaine) with powdered milk perhaps. Playing with Ralphie, the dog. Who knows.

Eventually, House Mother Normal picks up the phone. What. The wages, Shae says. It happens, House Mother Normal says. Your wages will be a few days late, also reduced. It's been a slow month. Shae hangs up. A slow month?! I cry, I make like my ribbon face. It didn't feel like a slow month (we couldn't have worked any faster).

But what's that—. (A synthetic hum.) What's what? (A growl.) There—in the back. (The ribbony tears hanging off of my sweater are like catnip to the lypard.) What if it's coming for us, I say. The lypard? Shae asks. It won't. The lypard is stealthy, it likes to blend in with its environment. The murky pink carpet with dots (stars) is not a night a lypard blends into. It'll stay in the background, that's my prediction. It'll tear through the recesses of the foyer, that's all. Are you sure, I say.

No, Shae admits, two days later. Not altogether. As a matter of fact, they're inclined to revise their risk assessment in light of the latest: Guests have started to disappear. (What?) The number of hotel guests checking in (staying) is significantly higher compared to the number of hotel guests checking out (paying). Take this one, Shae says, looking at our register. Checked in last week, never checked out. (Lypard or moonlight flit.) Or this one. (Made off without paying?)

A guest comes up to reception. Checking in, she says. The guest is wearing a bubblegum coloured jersey sweatshirt with a beige appliqué across the front. Name? I ask. Tonya Harding, she replies. T, O, N, Y, A? Yes. Harding—ok. Is there a public ice rink nearby? Tonya Harding wants to know. Ryde Arena, Shae replies. Shut by bailiffs in October '17. What was that, Tonya Harding says. What was what. Tonya Harding saw a fing tear through the foyer, apparently. (Bubblegum is like catnip to the lypard.) Probably nothing, I say. (Did it have a massive tear in its eye?) The light in here can play tricks on you, Shae says. Have the scaffolding removed, Tonya Harding suggests, let some daylight in. (The scaffolding is a permanent fixture, this is England, the scaffolding will outstay us all.) Here's your key, I say, your room's upstairs. Welcome to the New House of Normal, we hope you enjoy your stay. Tonya Harding retreats.

Shae and I look at each other. As a precaution, Shae says, let's heighten security. Let's turn the lights on. (The lypard is stealthy, it won't like the exposure.) Shae starts with the large and partially derelict Lee-Bul-style chandelier hanging from the very high ceiling. (Icicle-shaped mirror shards, diamantes, dangling silver chains and blocks of transparent acrylic, all stuck together into one big gaudy bauble—.) The chandelier works, that's surprising. Next, wall lamps. Desk lamps at reception, floor lamps in the lounge area—on. Still dingy. You know the Carpet Warehouse across the road? Shae asks. Not really a Carpet Warehouse—entrepreneurial indie using a version of the branded name illegitimately? Yes? Get more lights. Cheap lights. Ok, I'm off.

I return having spent a week's wages on lights. Fairy lights. A job lot of reject but 'perfectly functioning' IKEA work lamps. Fittings and light bulbs, extension leads. Let's do it, let's put them to work! We unwrap, set up, plug in, connect and switch—we are ON! We glow like a nuclear power plant. We are lit like Dungeness at night, has Christmas come early. This light will drive anything shy into hiding.

Hot topic—remember the Reebok Working Class Plus, the classic trainer? Its self-fulfilling prophecy? Cultural theorist Paul Willis (1977) argued that, to some extent, working-class school boys were complicit in the reproduction of their own class disadvantage. Working-class boys, Willis argued, and specifically the boys attending the 'Hammertown' Secondary School in the British Midlands, participated in a rebellious counterculture, successfully resisting the norms of capitalism transmitted in school. But their victory was, in Willis's terms, pyrrhic (ONE MORE SUCH VICTORY AND WE ARE LOST). Having done badly at school, the boys ended up having to take on lowly paid working-class jobs as adults.

'It's, uh, resenting authority I suppose.' 'No, I don't understand, you cunt' (to a teacher). 'Can I go home now please' (in mid-session). 'Today, I've learnt nothing.'

Moving out of '77 and into '97, the rebel is Shae (14). Shae Benet (14) is 60% boy and 100% bravado. One of the brightest and most popular kids in their year, they've got a failing academic record.

Ok, is this Shae's (14) prophecy self-fulfilling. (Yes. It is.)

If it weren't for the fact that—. What. If the other boys hadn't—. Hadn't what?! There is a twist.

The self-fulfilling of Shae's (14) prophecy is

somewhat impacted by the fact that the shoe (the Reeboks Working Class Plus) fits, but also doesn't: Shae is working-class and also queer (there's no hiding it). (Tommy Pico the poet is NDN and also queer.) Have the other boys turned on you (queer). Yes. Yes, they have. Compared to 'Hammertown' in the '70s, counter school cultures in North West London are more racially diverse in '97. But girls and homos are nonos. Girls and homos are—you can say that again. Counter school cultures are built on exclusions—Shae (15) gets dropped by their peers. So Shae (15) changes tack. Having left school with two GCSEs, Shae (16) starts grafting. Like, you wouldn't believe. Do you know why they're grafting like this. (Queer. Queerdo.) They're putting their difference to work—.

Is this how Shae (36) will escape their working-class destiny? (The Reebok Working Class Plus fits, but also doesn't?) Can Shae (36) mobilise some sort of cultural capital they've acquired through grafting, that sets them apart from their working-class peers? Will they work their way out of their job (*this* job)? The job's ok, don't get me wrong—a little less than dreamy, perhaps. (It's got its challenges.) There's scope for improvement, let's say. And Shae's got real potential. They're diamond, you see. And they're not getting any younger—.

You know PACCBET, the Russian design brand and collaborative effort between Gosha Rubchinskiy and friend Tolia Titaev? PACCBET, pronounced rassvyet, means 'dawn' in Russian. ('Dawn', not 'lit like a power plant during both, day and night'. Not 'lit like a high security prison complex'.)

Shae and I are in the foyer, moonlighting. We're planning on taking designer fashion to the people, specifically the yellow 'sunboy' design from PACCBET's debut collection. Shae is transferring the classic image onto plain yellow t-shirts via iron-on print technology. I'm attaching fake PACCBET labels to collars, I'm like a sewing machine.

Several labels in, and my skills are improving. I feel confident, I try alterations. Let's pad the sleeves of this t-shirt here (giving biceps). Let's add shoulder pads (upping back beef). Beef up the chest, too (*PECS*BET—hah! hah!). What you doing, Shae asks.

Me? Nothing.

Walter van Beirendonck's AW '13 collection included a jumper with horizontal stripes that curved round the wearer's midriff, creating the illusion of a gut. (Turning twinks into bears—.) In SS '02, Ann-Sofie Back showed a women's top with two breast-like pads sewed in at dropped (droopy) breast level. (Subverting normative body types through high fashion—.)

But were these collections viable, Shae asks. Did Ann-Sofie Back's tops fly off the shelves, yes or no. No, I admit. We need the t-shirt business to work, Shae insists. We need it to pay. Last month was 'slow', and that was before hotel guests have started to disappear (without paying). Comme, Westwood, they're getting paid—, I object. Can you get back to attaching labels please, Shae says.

I try a different approach. I explain that my fashion-forward take on the classic PACCBET design not only subverts normative body types, but double functions as some sort of protective wear, some sort of soft armour when handling big cats. (The extra padding.) Once I'll be able to buy it, the new cap will come in like a helmet. Also good—green metal frame shades with orange glasses (available also in grey and rose-tinted), offering protection against the indoors glare. The evolved 'sunboy' look I'm proposing responds directly to our environment, its distinct predators and, less obviously, the shift from natural to artificial lighting! This is future fashion at its most urgent, I say.

Comme des Garçons' Rei Kawakubo looks into the future of the silhouette with vast, voluminous dresses this season, combining leather and foam in all-white and belted gowns, covered with octopus-style suckers. What the clothes lack in wearability, they make up for in fierceness. What the clothes lack in affordability—sorry.

You won't be buying accessories (neither cap, nor eyewear) if our sideline won't come off the ground, Shae says. Ok, I say, let me show you something—. I put on my one-off *PECS*BET t-shirt and put my arm round Shae's shoulders. Despite, or maybe because of, the buff type I'm embodying, I'm giving off child with supernatural abilities levels of outsider weirdness. Weak on its own, but with Shae's working boi reenforcement, we are selling the look. I take pictures of us in the full-length mirror—the flash reflects at the height of my waist, left, and the Winter Wonderland we established, this being May, reflects everywhere. (Look, Shae! You telling me this won't sell—?) We post the pictures on the socials, captioned '#PACCBET #*PECS*BET #sunboy #artificiallightbois #Gosha #NewHouseofNormal #lypardproof #Comme'. Sale starts now.

Why do the English middle classes sound like they've come through the New York voguing and ballroom scene on social media, never mind.

The local youths are vaping outside Wimpy (the burger bar). It's cold and wet—still, they're in t-shirts. They're bored, they're rolling around on the pavement for kicks. Shae's in their parka, they're carrying a Tesco bag for life. They chat to the Wimpy kids, gesticulating. I watch from across the road. Shae unzips their parka, revealing their PACCBET t-shirt underneath. More chatting. Nodding. (Quality counterfeits—.) (Can't tell the difference, can you.) Shae pulls a small stash of t-shirts from their bag for life and hands them round. All of the male identified kids take one. Do you do crop? the female identified kids want to know. No. Sorry, we don't do crop—an oversight, and the result of the absence of a femme on our design team. (We commit to addressing the issue asap.) The male identified kids take off their own t-shirts, they try on ours. (Hold my vape.) (You got XXXL?) One of them bins his old t-shirt for effect. The others follow suit. At £4 a t, they are buying. (I'll have two.) (Four!) (How are they flush? I wonder.) The female identified kids lose interest (no crop), I don't blame them. They are back on the floor, dragging each others' hair through the dirt, making the most of their environment and position within it.

Shae and I continue along the High Street towards Ryde Harbour. Once a Regency seaside resort, visitor numbers in Ryde were up and down historically, then down for good 1970s onwards (cheap Mediterranean charter flights). With the exception of its young, present-day Ryde is unaspirational in all respects. The Georgian buildings look like they could do with a few quid being thrown at them. The people look like they're on their last penny. There's a Sainsbury's, charity shops, an electrical goods store. Hotels. Estate agents, pubs, the exotic pets shop—. Wait, is this a gay bar? No. We should have gone north (Glasgow or Manchester), I say. I've got family down here, Shae replies. Ah ok. What family.

There's Ryde Harbour, the ferry and hovercraft terminals. Souvenir shops, Minghella ices (closed out of season). A group of construction workers are sitting on a bench. Shae goes up. They unzip their parka, showcasing their t-shirt on their own flat-chested body. How vulnerable they are, I think. But Shae is fine (their binding is tight, and their London working-class accent is not dissimilar to the Portsmouth working-class accent). Shae chats and points at me. I wave. (I'm wearing the *PECS*BET t-shirt under my overcoat, the big ticket item. No way am I taking my coat off, no way.) The construction workers don't return my wave. Instead, they stare. (Is it a boy or a girl. Child or adult, what is it.) They prefer to deal with the boy (Shae). Shae agrees a few sales (4 x XL). Good—t-shirt business is good. This will keep us afloat.

RAUSCHENBERG AND BREXIT ARE BRAVING THE SURF

We have fighter planes rockets explosions on our sweaters, this is not *Top Gun*, this is not an haute couture fashion show. This is the Isle of Wight off the south coast of England, the beach outside Ryde. Shae is wearing their military green parka over their sweater, it's parka weather in June. Black oversize joggers, white Reebok classic trainers. The Isle of Wight is home to the British space rocket industry and Her Majesty's high security prison complex (HMP Parkhurst). There's Ryde Arena (the boarded up ice rink) and Sandown Zoo. Sandown Zoo?! Yes, and British beaches. Shae is looking for their parent, apparently. Their mother, their father, it's all relative. As far as Shae can tell, their parent is not on the beach. They think that their parent is more likely in HMP Parkhurst than on the beach. Unless there's an Aldi in Ryde? (Aldi alcohol is Shae's parent's food, apparently.) (Affordable bubbly—.)

Robert Rauschenberg's *Mud Muse* (1968-71) is a 12ft by 9ft glass and aluminium tank with bubbling bentonite clay inside. The tank is equipped with microphones and a tape machine recording the bubbling, which in turn (in play mode) triggers a system of pumps inciting new bentonite (benny) activity. Rauschenberg's piece is in a museum in London, what's it got to do with Isle of Wight beach life. The tide is low, the ground is wet, the terrain is launching bentonite missiles, that's what.

The local MP is delighted with the EU referendum result. The Isle of Wight voted 62% in favour of leaving the European Union. ('We have done it— voted to Leave—, and that is all we can do.') Bullet rain from the terrain upwards, is this a natural event or a case of national politics? WHAM! BAM! A projectile hits Shae on the shoulder. We retaliate, FIGHTER PLANES ROCKETS EXPLOSIONS ARE GOING OFF,THEY REALLY ARE GOING OFF NOW, WE ARE NOT WEARING OUR SWEATERS FOR NO REASON. As if connected via a hidden tape machine, benny activity on the ground is increasing proportionally.

Over there, I say. Is it your parent? Stuck in a black and white car tyre, Rauschenberg's taxidermy merino sheep (*Monogram*, 1955-59), like us, is dodging bentonite bullets. Shae isn't sure about this one, they are going to have to take a closer look. On inspection, *Monogram* (Money) is reminding Shae not of their parent, but the Isle of Wight's Brexit-done, Brexit-doing MP. The way it's stuck in its black and white tyre—. But Shae, I say. It's got rainbow coloured acrylics all over its face. Money is gay (flying the rainbow face). Still, Shae says. Rainbow or not, they aren't convinced of Money's pro-European orientation. They think we might be dealing with a representative of the UKIP or English Defence League LGBTQI+ divisions. The rise of the UKIP or English Defence League LGBTQI+ divisions is not a joke, it is very serious. Shae thinks we should leave Money on the beach where we found it on the grounds of its potential links to right wing LGBTQI+ organisations.

Benny missiles are flying, they are airborne like starlings, I've hated the intimation of paintballing from the beginning. WHAMBAM! Another hit, echoing Shae's t-shirt with the pink-mouthed shark, black and white stripy flashes and blood dripping from the hem upwards. WHAMBAM! it says on said t-shirt which Shae isn't wearing, not under their sweater, and never with their black oversize joggers. The pink-mouthed shark rises from the sea surfing a tidal wave. What if this part of the beach were about to get flooded. (This isn't an haute couture fashion show and this isn't a surfer's paradise.) Already the water is rising, Shae's Reeboks are drenched. Let's go, I say. Hang on——. Shae just wants to make sure their parent isn't over there. Where? There——! The pink-mouthed shark releases a black and white stripy lightning bolt from its eye. The lightning bolt travels across the left-hand side of the t-shirt including the sleeve, creating a zebraesque dreamworld. It's raining, I complain. But Shae will not be slowed down by the rain, this is England, Shae is British (second gen).

In the 1950s and '60s, the British space rocket programme saw the Isle of Wight's Needles Headland transformed into a real-life double-o seven film. British space rockets were assembled in underground workshops, apparently, then launched into the atmosphere from the Needles rocket testing site (like fireworks). I want an astronaut who is not Tim Peake (Mae Jemison, or Helen Sharman). What's that over there? I ask. (Shae's parent? No.)

On the Esplanade, a demonstration is building momentum. Local party activists are flying the rainbow flag. Some are carrying placards: 'Some gays vote UKIP. Get over it.' 'Don't let bigots enter our country.' 'Britain First!' The party activists are young working-class gays, twenty-somethings. They look just like Justin Bieber, only paler (white British).

They own Staffies named Judo, or Karate. They are good gays, community-orientated gays. Like me, they advocate PrEP. Unlike me, they blame Muslims for anti-gay sentiment on the island. They think Muslim culture is inherently homophobic hence incompatible with Western ideas. They're not racist (they say), they're progressive. They're caught up in the same eternal shitshow ('discourse') as the rest of us, positioning the 'liberal' West against the 'primitive' East (what Edward Said said, and, later, Jasbir Puar). This view originates in the upper spheres of British imperial society (NOT the white working classes), and it is currently peddled by the ultra-posh Tory government (and Peter Tatchell) with renewed vigour.

Shae doesn't smile, I don't smile, we are migrants from North West London. We roll out the tanks on our sweaters and make straight for the Esplanade.

What if the earth were riddled with microphones. What if a tape machine were recording the tracks of our tanks, what if (on playback) a hole opened up under the Esplanade and swallowed the demonstration. What if a pink-mouthed shark rode in on a tidal wave, what if a b&w lightning bolt from its eye turned the scene into a zebraesque fantasy. But this isn't an art installation, this isn't a motif on a t-shirt. This is the Isle of Wight off the south coast of

England, this is what we are faced with.

I'm in the kitchen working flat out. I make to prepare squid ink tagliatelle at large volume. (I still can't cook.) Sandy refuse is collecting in the bucket, it's raining black squid ink. Counting the hours, I'm sticking cocktail umbrellas into Styrofoam—. One. Two. Three.

Five. I'm nowhere near done. What if I got myself out of here. Can I? I can. Eleven from *Stranger Things* has psychokinetic abilities, she can access other dimensions—. Flick. I'm on a beach. What beach. Not Ryde—Shanklin? Not Shanklin. I don't know this beach. No British seaside chill, it's atypically balmy. Sun-bleached beach parasols, and not a cocktail umbrella in sight. What's this yipping, hurrahing? The reeboks are braving the surf, the polar bears are savaging the ice cream vendor. Beach life, *this* beach life, is dreamy, this is different dimension type stuff—.

A letter from the UK Home Office lies on a sun lounger like a German beach towel. For me? I open the letter. It's my permanent residence card! I rub the flimsy blue cardboard foldout with my finger, the print comes off. Squid gut gets on it, thing is disintegrating—. *Keep the document in a safe place*, the accompanying letter advises. *The Home Office does not retain any records of your residence status.*

Shae. Where's Shae? I go looking for Shae up

and down the happy beach. There they are—SHAE! Shae looks 30 years older than Shae. Iller. Shae?! No. Not Shae. The person I found in this here dimension is Shae's parent, apparently (the cocktail umbrella to Shae's beach parasol). Do you know where Shae is? I ask. No, Shae's parent replies. I never know where Shae is. (Clanking bottles.) You got something for me? Shae's parent asks. Like, what? (Aldi alcohol. Affordable bubbly.) No, I say. Look—I'm going to see Shae. Yes, Shae. They're in Ryde. R, Y, D, E. They're looking for you. Want to come? Come—, Shae's parent echoes, they go blank. I can tell I have lost them. I can't wait, I'm off.

The electric light goes on (it is necessary at 11am). I'm back in my kitchen—there's Shae, serving up sunboy flair and I'm here for it. You'll never guess, I say, flashing my permanent residence card.

Same day, only later. Shae and I are in the foyer, staffing reception. We're watching TV on Shae's tablet. Some BBC drama, they're so violent now. Tonight's drama has incredible lions in it, they are nauseous for some reason. (Were the squid ink tagliatelle on the turn?) My parent communicates with me via the electrics, Shae says. Email? I ask. The lights, Shae replies. See the flicker over there? On. Off. On off. ONOFFONOFFONOFF. Dodgy electrics, I say. Power surges. But Shae insists their parent is speaking to them from wherever they are. (Not Ryde. Not Shanklin.) Ok, the glare in the foyer intensifies. Then all of the lamps go off at the exact same time. Then the desk lamps at reception come on. The lamp by the bottom of the stairs, the one a flight further up, the one at the top of the second flight of stairs—come on, in successive order. Now the light on the top landing comes on, this one flickers. Flickers again. Then the big Lee Bul chandelier hanging off of the tower's ceiling starts beaming violently. (The daylights really are living—.) The chandelier goes off—and the light starts travelling downwards, much more rapidly than it went up, as if falling. (Fa–thud.) Darkness. Shae? I say. Yes—. As suddenly as they started playing up, the lights in the foyer return to normal (permanent day). What was that? I ask. (A cry for help?) (A SUICIDE NOTE?) Ok, I say. I look at Shae. (It's ok.) We agree on the fact that the light show meant probably nothing.

Nisha Ramayya the poet read a poem at Oxford once. Unlike the light show, it meant a lot. The poem had nauseous lions in it, they vomit (yes). Their vomit is astonishing, it has astonishing properties, it rises into the air where the distinct streams meet and create a flying vomit heart. It sounds like *My Little Pony* when I say it, but Ramayya said it beautifully.

So beautifully, in fact, that the image will stay with me for a long time—UNLIKE THE GUEST IN THE BUBBLEGUM JERSEY SWEATER WITH THE BEIGE APPLIQUÉ ACROSS THE FRONT WHO HAS ALREADY DISAPPEARED (without paying).

How can this be?! It can't be the terrible lypard's doing—? Except the odd outage (Shae's parent communicating), it's day in here 24 7! Daylight plus, even. Intolerable conditions for a shy predator, isn't that the idea. But Tonya Harding is not in the foyer, and neither is she upstairs. (What if it gets them in their beds at night.) (Its natural habitat is the foyer, it hates upstairs.) What about Tonya Harding's belongings? Gone. GONE? (Moonlight flit.) (The lypard is smart, it removes traces. It feasts on incriminatory evidence.)

THEY TRAVELLED AROUND ON FOUR SUCTION CUPS, WERE SMALL, AND LOOKED FURRY

It's Gay Pride Black Pride Trans Pride Gay Shame Queer Picnic in London. On the Isle of Wight, I search 'how to build a parade float'. I click on a post on author Dennis Cooper's blog on precisely this topic. The blog says to begin planning several months before the day of the parade. (What parade.) What parade, Shae asks. Ok, we are working within a compressed time-frame, I say. *Form a committee consisting of 5 to 6 people and design the float.* Let's see. The reeboks (1, 2), the polar bears (3, 4+), Shae (5) and I, that makes 6+. (The number of polar bears fluctuates, their numbers are up and down up and down.) *In terms of design, convey a simple but powerful message.* Message, wt message. What message, I ask.

Shae doesn't reply, they are reading. They are wearing their t-shirt with the pink-mouthed shark, black and white stripy flashes, and blood dripping from the hem upwards. *The float should leave an enchanting memory and positive message with the crowd and social media users*, it says on the blog. It strikes me that Shae in their t-shirt is not conveying a positive message. Shae, I say, listen: *Animals and other props should not be threatening*—. Shae says they're not a parade float, just showboating. (Out of everyone, only the polar bears laugh.) But it says on Dennis Cooper's blog—, I insist. Shae says they wouldn't want to leave enchanting memories with hypothetical parade goers. They're wearing their shark t-shirt IN PROTEST, and that's the message they'd like to convey. Oh, I say (oh, ok). (I get it.) My float, too, is a protest! My float is a direct response to the UKIP, the English Defence League demo, reality check! Animals and other props should be threatening maybe, I say. Dennis Cooper would back me on this, I have a feeling.

Next, you will need paint, preferably rainbow colours, to enhance the visibility of your float. Basic decorating skills are essential. Shae? I say. No answer. (Shae's reading again.) Shae! What, Shae says. Paint, I say. Lots of paint in the basement, Shae says. Left there when the renovation of the building stalled in 2009, apparently (along with the scaffolding). What colours? I ask. Grey, Shae replies. Grey—? Just grey? (Since our encounter with the UKIP and English Defence League LGBTQI+ divisions, Shae and I have developed an allergy to the rainbow palette— but grey?) I'll skip the paint stage, Dennis Cooper's blog, no hard feelings.

(Is that a dog yapping upstairs?) (Loud barking.) Did you hear that? I ask. House Mother Normal's dog, Ralphie, Shae says.

At some point, we'll need a 4-wheel flatbed trailer, I say. Anyone?! 4-wheel flatbed trailer? What about this, the pink felt mobile notice board in the reception area. Take it apart, flip the vertical part—might that work? Shae? Shae! What! Shae snaps. They are reading, in case I hadn't noticed. (So am I—Dennis Cooper's blog.) Shae is reading Samuel Delany (not Beckett), apparently, specifically a novelette, *The Star Pit* (1967), about a group of mechanics in an intergalactic garage servicing the starships of an upper class. Shae says they identify with *The Star Pit*'s protagonist to an extent (a mechanic). (Content Warning: alienation, alcoholism, social oppression.) They want to stay with the story—.

Once you begin building the float, involve a STELLAR MECHANIC, I say. Not that it says to 'involve a stellar mechanic' on Dennis Cooper's blog—I'm segueing into Delany to get Shae on board. Ok,

Shae sighs, putting down their Delany. They proceed to ask the polar bears and the reeboks to present what, if anything, they have come up with in terms of parade float development. The polar bears have drawn up an elaborate starship design, disregarding Dennis Cooper's advice to keep it simple. It's the 'DON'T Do It Yourself' section of the blog which has piqued their interest (*Let Floatasia Parade Float Co. build your ambitious design*). Floatasia operate on the IoW? Or just Iowa? Shae looks at the polar bears (sheer disbelief). What planet are you on? Next! The reeboks have invented a name for our float: *FLAOT*. (They are the kind of poets calling a poem *PEOM*, or *POME*.) That's as far as they got. (Traipsing upstairs. Doggy paws—. We might be on borrowed time, you know—.)

All morning in Practical Theory (a ridiculous name for a ridiculous class) we'd been putting together a model-keeler intergalactic drive—. For Delany (as for Cooper), the emphasis is on *practical*. Without further ado, Shae goes over to the lounge area and tears the upholstery apart. Demolishing the four-seater sofa, they are procuring (very) raw material for building a model-keeler parade float. We are working with urgency now—*psychological freaks with some hormone imbalance in their systems*—and without a plan. Stapler, Shae says. Hammer! Polar bears, can you just—*they travelled around on four suction cups when using kinetic motion for ordinary traversal of space, were small, and looked furry*—fetch the hot glue gun. That's it, get right underneath. Put some glue there there and there. That'll do. Looks intergalactic to me—let's heave it onto the reception desk. One two three, GO!

The polar bears, the reeboks, Shae and I GET! ON! BOARD! our float (we climb onto the reception desk). Space-flying, non-complying, we are one hot bloody mess. (*When designing the float, remember not to overcrowd it.*) Our float is the sink hole that never opened under the Esplanade and that never stopped the march of the nationalists. Our float is the anti-UKIP, anti-EDL demonstration and a full-body protest against Britain First. Our float is a launch pad for migrants—it doesn't have wheels and it will not get painted.

We are in the process of nailing our colours to the mast (Shae's WHAMBAM t-shirt), when House Mother Normal comes down the stairs. Good lord, she's got Ralphie with her—a Labrador of calf-size proportions. WHAT'S HAPPENING (Normal). Grrr (Ralphie). What's with the sofa?! The reception desk? And the lights?! Is this the illuminations, am I in Blackpool?!! And omg is it back to work for Shae and I. And I mean NOW—House Mother Normal tolerates zero delay delany Delany. You can finish your book later, she says to Shae. Reading, she says, is for the underemployed.

Later on Newsnight, the Prime Minister is wearing a bracelet depicting an artist with a disability. What possesses the PM to commodify an artist with a disability, while under her leadership UK disability rights have been declared a humanitarian catastrophe by the United Nations, is quite unclear. Handling a sharp kitchen knife, I'm scouring bloody beaches off the insides of squid. (I'm making squid bouillabaisse, fingers crossed.) Shae looks up from their tablet (Newsnight). They say they've got news of their own. News, wt news.

The reeboks are scaling the kitchen work surface, they are not allowed on there for good reasons (food hygiene). Ok, I make an exception, the reeboks are allowed to sit on the red chopping board there (red for raw meat). Now the polar bears, too, climb up. Sit on the blue chopping board, I say, blue for fish. Tory blue. Traditionally, the Tory Party's colour has been blue but the Prime Minister has taken to wearing a lot of commie red. What possesses the PM to commodify commie red is also unclear.

Breaking: Money's here. Who? Money, Shae repeats. Someone left Robert Rauschenberg's taxidermy merino sheep (*Monogram*, 1955-59) outside the main entrance, apparently. (What.) (Is this a threat?) Shae says they took action immediately, they took Money in. In, where? I ask. In here, Shae replies. Where, the pantry? God, yes. There's Money. Look at the state of it (Money). What happened to its face?! THE ST. GEORGE'S CROSS HAS BEEN PAINTED ONTO THE FACE OF THE AMERICAN SHEEP.

During *Theater Piece No. 1* (1952), a multimedia performance by Robert Rauschenberg et el at Black Mountain College in North Carolina, four white canvasses (*White Paintings,* 1951) were suspended from the ceiling in the shape of a cross. The St. George's cross? What? No! As for Money—Shae still can't decide whether Money is a survivor (one of us), or a perpetrator with links to right-wing LGBTQI+ organisations and on that basis, an intruder and spy.

Something something British lion, Shae's tablet says. An ex-foreign minister on Newsnight now, all the top players. RAAAhAWR! But what's this, the roar of a British lion? It's House Mother Normal, careering down the corridor—! SHAE, QUEEECK! GET MONEY OUT OF HERE, QUEEECK! If House Mother Normal sees Money—or the reeboks, the polar bears, for that matter—I'll have had it (wildlife contaminating the catering environment). Shae snatches Money, they exit through the back door. Here's House Mother Normal. Ralphie, sit.

Sit! No, sit by the door! What is it, Ralphie? (Dog won't sit still, it's the scent of Money driving him wild.) Now House Mother Normal is talking to me. I can't concentrate on anything she is saying. UKIP, the EDL, Britain First—they know where we are, is all I can think. Address, everything. I look down onto my Styrofoam box containing raw squid on inky ice, and feel foreign.

Today is my Life in the UK test. Like the permanent residence card, the Life in the UK test certificate is a requirement when applying for British citizenship by naturalisation. I arrive 30 minutes ahead of time at the test centre in Newport. I ring the buzzer. Through the intercom I'm instructed to wait outside. Waiting outside in the rain brings back memories of Citizens Advice Bureaus '99-'02, never mind.

The test centre's interior, too, reminds me of Citizens Advice Bureaus. Bad air. Too hot. Us, the disenfranchised. The actual test takes place in an open plan office space with fourteen 'work stations', 'separated' by flimsy partition screens. I sit down. *Before you begin the test, read the instructions*, it says on the computer screen. I skim the instructions. Motivated by a sense of injustice (fury), I race through 24 multiple choice questions. I tell myself to slow down—there are trick questions. (Like *Who*

Wrote 'The Daffodil'? (1) William Blake (2) Robert Browning (3) William Wordsworth (4) None of them. Correct answer: (4) None of them. William Wordsworth wrote a lyric poem called 'The Daffodils', plural, NOT 'The Daffodil', singular. Or *Who fought who during the Hundred Year War? (1) English kings fought the French. (2) Boudicca, queen of the Iceni, defeated the Romans. (3) King Kenneth MacAlpin beheaded Prince Sutton Hoo. (4) The Hundred Year War did not last a hundred years but a hundred and sixteen years in total. Correct answer: (1) English kings fought the French. (4) The Hundred Year War did not last a hundred years but a hundred and sixteen years in total is also true, but incorrect in relation to the question.*)

I'm out, waiting to hear my result. (The test is primarily designed to test a particular form of educational capital, namely the ability to memorise information—kings, queens, invasions, a sanctioned version of British history and culture.) 21 out of 24 questions correct, I passed. (It's an intelligence test!) I'm handed the coveted certificate unceremoniously—a plain piece of printed out paper. *Keep this certificate in a safe place*, it says. *The test centre does not retain records of test outcomes.* What is it with the Home Office and safe places, they really have no idea.

DRUGS ARE A THING OF THE PAST WE ARE NOT HIGH ON LIFE

What's the Wimpy kid doing in the foyer. There's another one. Two in total. Hi—. They don't stop for Shae and I, they head straight upstairs to House Mother Normal's floor. Minutes later, they're back down. They've got Ralphie on a leash. What you doing, Shae asks. Walking the dog. (They smirk.) Ralphie is licking my leg, I'm not keen. What you got in those Tesco bags? Shae asks. (Jangling. Rustling.) (Bags of tablets—pound bags.) NOTHING, the Wimpy kid says. (Aaaaahahaha—'nothing'!) (Laced barbiturates, fresh from the tablet press.) What's funny, I ask. RALPHIE, GET OFF ME—. (That dog.) Come on, Ralph, let's go. The Wimpy kids leave, walking Ralphie to Ryde Harbour, apparently. Ten fifteen minutes, and they're back. No pound bags now. Just a small bag of something (unadulterated raw material). Bracing walk? Shae asks. The Wimpy kids give Shae the inside out V (fuck you), the ok gesture (arsehole). They take Ralphie upstairs. A minute later, one of them comes back down. Got any washing powder? No. Aspirin? Anything lends itself to being pulverised? No! Wimpy k pulls a face and heads for the shops. Returns with a packet of Persil. Heads upstairs. Back down in the foyer within ten, or is that the other kid. Shae Benet? this one asks. Who's asking, Shae asks in turn. The teenager slips Shae a sachet. For your parent, with regards from House Mother Normal. My parent? Shae echoes. But—. Just doing as I'm told, Wimpy k shrugs. Take the £ before you hand over.

Drugs are a thing of the past, Shae and I are not high on anything. We are not high on life. Meanwhile, the reeboks are tripping on *TR&YN* (2016), the queer techno medieval poem by Jay Bernard. At one point in the book, *TR&YN*'s protagonist is being ingested by something, a dinosaur, who thought the protagonist *looked pretty hot (in the chicken wings sense of hot). Squeezed through the dino's intestines*, *TR&YN*'s protagonist *undergoes not a transition, exactly*, but an equally radical transformation. The reeboks say they identify with the dinosaur in Jay Bernard's *TR&YN*. As poets, they find that they, too, are catalysts for transformation. Shae looks at the reeboks, they think they have lost it. You think your poetry is transformational? Are you high? Got to be honest wt u, not really. According to Shae, protest, not poetry, has the transformational power of a dino's digestive tract. If anything, Shae identifies with *TR&YN*'s protagonist. They feel like they're being put through the wringer a lot, albeit in their own post-austerity, Isle-of-Wight-living, crisis-managing reality and environment.

It's a day of protest in Ryde (Gay Pride Black Pride Trans Pride Gay Shame Queer Picnic). Instead of a fully executed float, we are parading the pink felt mobile notice board down the Esplanade. Look at this mobile notice board here, Shae says to the reeboks. Signal pink. This is how to get out a message, effect sociopolitical change—.

The sand is peachy and so is the sea, and yet it's just us on the Esplanade. We expected this to be rush hour, but no. The people of Ryde are not going to work at this hour (8.30am). Unemployment on the Isle of Wight is absolutely horrendous, the BBC reported in 2011, 2016 and again in 2019. 4.9% of working age people are claiming Job Seeker's Allowance, compared with 3.6% in Southampton and 3.8% in Portsmouth. A poetry pamphlet has more readers than our parade has spectators, I say.

Shae looks at me. (But it's true—!) At this rate, our protest won't be changing hearts and minds, nor will it be effecting sociopolitical change. How to mobilise the masses if there's no one around—?

Then this happens: ROOOOAAAAARRRR! This is not a British lion, this is Shae stepping up their demonstration game. (Losing it.) POOORTSMOUTH! Portsmouth, can you see us over there?! Signal pink! No response. WAKE UP POMPEY!! Determined that someone, Portsmouth, will notice us, Shae is firing missiles (stones) into the Solent. But what's this—Shae spots the pink-mouthed shark in the distance (that's the shark from Shae's t-shirt). SHARKAAEEE, Shae cries, OVER HERE! We want transformational politics! We want change!

Personally, I'm inclined to exercise caution re Sharkae. Judging from our last trip to the beach, we don't know, exactly, whether it's friendly or not. Too late. Sharkae comes to a halt in the shallow in front of us. Shae, Sharkae says. (What trip is this.) Articulate a singular demand (one), and I'll take care of it. Be specific.

Put on the spot, Shae can't decide which of their many concerns they want Sharkae to take care of most urgently. A demand, to who? The government? Anyone, Sharkae replies. Stop warmongering?

LGBTQI+ to the front? Worker's rights? A pro-immigration agenda? Social housing in London? A lypard tamer for every household? Tories out?! I can't choose just one, we have intersecting demands—.

The blood on Shae's t-shirt is starting to boil, it's rising more urgently than it usually does. The black and white stripy lightning bolt creeps into Shae's field of vision—they settle for climate change. (What.) (We've got the English Defence League at our doorstep and Shae says to end climate change?) (This goes to the polar bears who are not out campaigning this morning. This one's for you—.) Ok I'll end climate change, Sharkae says. But first, Sharkae wants Shae to address their internalised anger issues. Firing missiles into the Solent like that—. Sharkae thinks that Shae's anger against Portsmouth would be better directed against their absent parent. Come again? Shae says. This is unreal, is the shark a psychoanalyst—? Shae does not rule out completely that they might be angry with their absent parent, but they don't think that this is the time nor the place to psychologise. This is a political site. Hang on—this WOULD be a political site if SOMEBODY ANYBODY THE PEOPLE OF RYDE OR OF PORTSMOUTH paid ANY ATTENTION to our EXQUISITELY CRAFTED FELT MOBILE NOTICE BOARD HERE! Heart-felt, even. The blood on Shae's t-shirt is boiling properly now, it's practically foaming at the mouth. I see, Sharkae replies. Since you insist on deferring psychotherapy, I'll end climate change later. Sharkae is being a bit bloody-minded now. Blood-thirsty, even. The pinks and the blood co-conspire, they co-produce a black and white stripy lighting storm, signalling feeding season for sharks. Sharkae can't help itself, it attacks the jurassic transformation machine in Jay Bernard's *TR&YN*. It tears into the dinosaur's flanks, it savages things—. This isn't the drugs talking, we are not high on life. On Ryde beach, sharks kill transformation machines and protest has no transformational power.

Shae suggests we call the Minister for Loneliness, Tracey Crouch MP. We are calling to let you know we have hit an all-time low.

Who turned the lights off? (Shae's parent? No. House Mother Normal.) When Shae and I get back, House Mother Normal is staffing reception. Ralphie is lying by her feet. Ah! House Mother Normal says, perfect timing. House Mother Normal just had a prepayment electricity meter installed. Here's your electricity key, thirty quid on it. Make it last. No Christmas lights in July, nor December, for that matter. Shae and I look at each other. Ok—. (The lights were on for a reason.) House Mother Normal has been reading the business accounts against the guest register on Shae's tablet, they look wrong. When did this one check out (Tonya Harding). Harding? Shae looks at the register on the tablet. Not yet. (Never.) What you mean—'not yet'. They only booked for one night, weeks ago. They disappeared, Shae admits. Do explain, House Mother Normal says. Even better, let ME explain the JOYS of a positive account balance. You do know what happens if guests 'disappear' without paying? Exactly, the deficit comes out of your wages. But what's that, do I have to get pest control in? Jesus, it's huge! Shae, did you see that? (The lypard.) Ralphie, go get it. Attack, Ralphie. No, ATTACK! Ralphie does not go in for the kill, he gets up and goes straight upstairs. Dog is a chicken, really. Normal—, Shae says. House Mother Normal does not want to hear. She wants to sit in the dark with the tablet and fiddle the accounts 'til they're joyful, for once. Normal, Shae tries again, I wouldn't recommend—. (THE LIGHTS WERE ON FOR A REASON.) But House Mother Normal's preoccupied with optional wage cuts, pulling tricks, cutting corners and profiteering. There is nothing for Shae and I but to leave her there and go about our work (cleaning the bedrooms, kitchen prep). When we return to the foyer at the end of our shifts, House Mother Normal is gone.

I'm in the doghouse, you know. I bought an artwork off the internet, it's just been delivered. It's a painting of a blond child on brown background, defaced with the slogan 'IT GETS WORSE'. A Christmas present to myself (this being August). Really? Shae says. How much? Shae is concerned about my high levels of spending. What's left of our wages—July, too, was deemed slow—has been going on electricity keys. In my defence, I thought the painting would look good in the foyer. I thought it would lift the foyer with its truth ('IT GETS WORSE'), its humour. I like Debbie (the blond child looks like a Debbie). She looks like the kind of boy that gets bullied at school on account of her effeminacy. I relate to what I imagine are the typically high levels of taunting and bullying Debbie experiences growing up gay on the Isle of Wight (or, wherever, Surrey). But Shae doesn't think I can afford to buy art (£90 excl. shipping). Not ever, really, but never less so than now—.

Today's the big day, you know. Half a year after obtaining my permanent residence status I am ready to submit my online application for British citizenship by naturalisation. I recorded my biometric information at the post office, I compiled NHS letters, bank statements and utility bills dated the year I first entered the country (evidence of my life in Britain). I passed a language test, the Life in the UK test, I produced my most substantial piece of creative writing to date (the online application form). On submitting (tonight), I'll be due to pay a grand and a half. I'm gna put it on a credit card, I say. Don't, Shae says. Really. Don't. Then HOW? I ask. You tell me—.

IT GETS WORSE, Debbie says, sparkly-eyed, and the universe (Ryde) is quick to respond.

Knock knock. (Is it the English Defence League. No.) (The local police searching for Tonya Harding? No!) It's the Isle of Wight immigration enforcement unit, four officers in the foyer. Can I help? Shae asks. Routine check. Tipped off by a neighbour. (What now, routine check or tip off?) Your passports please, the immigration enforcement officer says. Yes, ok. Shae is British (2nd gen), I'm European, all will be well. Shae hands their passport to the immigration officer. The officer double-checks Shae's photo, Shae's legal gender (female). He looks at Shae (boi). He looks at the photo again. (Freak.) Expires next year, the officer says, returning Shae's passport (ok). My turn, I hand over my permanent residence card. What's this, Mickey Mouse magazine? (What?) It's not a valid residence card, the officer says. But—, I say, I'm confused. According to the immigration enforcement officer, my permanent residence card isn't authentic, it has not been issued by the UK

Home Office. (Not issued by the UK Home Office? Who issued it? Thing slipped in from another dimension?!) PASSPORT, the officer reiterates. I fetch my European (EU) passport. I hand it to the officer, he scrutinises it. He scrapes plastic with his fingernail. Ok, he says, he returns my passport. All clear—FOR NOW. The officers chuckle ('for now'). (Get packing, hah hah.) The immigration enforcement unit is about to depart when—.

What's this. One of the officers is looking around the reception area. What's what. *This*. Behind the reception desk. Something—yellow. (Oh no.) (A folded up stash of counterfeit PACCBET t-shirts, ready to go.) The officer bends down. (Don't.) (The contravention of the 1981 Counterfeit Act is punishable by a suspended jail sentence.) The officer makes to pull out—. (DON'T.)

I act fast. I visualise Nisha Ramayya's vomit heart IT IS RISING UP THE ART DECO TOWER I TURN IT INTO A LASSO WITH MY OUTSIDER MIND! I throw the lasso, I catch and pull back the officer's hand—zap! The officer tries again. Again, I pull back. Wt!? Losing control of his motor responses isn't something the officer has experienced before—. (My lasso is invisible to the untrained eye.) The officer reaches with his other hand, I throw I pull back! I sprain his left shoulder.

(Ouch.) Another officer leaps to the rescue, I get this one round the neck. I pull—snap. He, too, gets hurt.

Shae looks at me (stop it). What, I mouth. You're making it worse, Shae mouths. I? I'm making it worse? This is all Debbie's fault! Since her arrival, things have GOTTEN WORSE. AND WORSE. AND WORSE! But ok, I drop the lasso.

My eczema flares up in real time, the back of my knees the insides of my wrists. Eleven from *Stranger Things* gets nosebleeds when she uses her telekinetic abilities, I get eczema all of the time.

The two remaining officers take over the search, they are like the police (equipped with enhanced search and seizure powers). They seize fifty or so counterfeit PACCBET t-shirts, also clothes labels, sewing needles, polyester thread, iron-on sunboy prints and an unopened pack of plain yellow t-shirts. (What we got here.) (Sideline, is it.) (Grafty.) They ask to speak to the owner of the establishment. Absentee proprietor, Shae replies. The manager? Ah, House Mother Normal. Indisposed, Shae says. (Disappeared.) (What if they searched House Mother Normal's space upstairs—.) (What if they frisked Shae, sachet of barbies in their back pocket. They're not mine, they're for my parent. Your parent. *Really*.) But the Isle of Wight immigration enforcement unit has had enough of us (freaks, freak hotel, did you see that freaky painting, let's get you to A&E—). Contravention of the 1981 Counterfeit Act is punishable by a suspended jail sentence, but this is more like a grand or so penalty notice. ('S all cash in the kitty). Pay now? Now?! Ok, later. The officers leave.

Ok ok, I say. Debbie was one big mistake! I've come to believe that Debbie is the kind of boy who will respond to the high levels of bullying she is exposed to growing up on the Isle of Wight by turning Tory in adult life! Shae? Shae! But Shae isn't even looking at me. This isn't about Debbie, apparently. Neither is it about me lassoing immigration officers. This is about my application for British citizenship which I will not be submitting, not later today, not anytime soon—NOT WITHOUT A VALID RESIDENCE CARD I WON'T. What is this pesky, disintegrating, squid inky, blue cardboard foldout you got, Shae says, if not a permanent residence card? Good question, I say, I don't know. I'm still in the doghouse, you know, and I have the feeling I'll be here a little while yet.

Shae's parent has issued another suicide note which is the surest sign that they're still alive.

The reeboks are dead, their bodies splayed out on the reception desk. (Is there a suicide note? No. I mean, yes, but it's from Shae's parent.) The polar bears are licking the reeboks' wounds, is this their way of grieving. Two hotel guests come up to reception. Eugh! Wt's this? The guests find the bodies on the reception desk—the polar bears' licking—disturbing, mildly put. Are they dead? the guests ask. Checking out? I ask in turn. Please, the guests confirm. Was everything alright for you? I ask. So so, they reply. The food wasn't great. Also, this—. The polar bears are licking increasingly frantically— are they swallowing?! Don't! Spit that out! I hold the polar bears at bay with the back of my hand when—WHOOAAA!! What?! The guests' FACES when the reeboks—MOVE!!! First one leg, then another. A tail and a head. Turns out, the reeboks were alive all along. They were just playing! They get up, they stagger, they fall over like Domino pieces. Domino's Pizza?! The guests are aghast. Here we go—they ask to speak to the manager. No, not Shae. THE MANAGER, House Mother Normal. But they were just playing, I say, defending the reeboks. This isn't a playground, the guests retort. This is the foyer of an admittedly substandard hotel, this is slap bang in the middle of the reception desk—. Here's Shae now. What's going on, Shae asks. They want Normal, I say. Normal? Why? I point (the reeboks). The reeboks are back on their BS—playing dead, lying around like wrongly aligned Domino pieces.

You know Fred Wah's autofiction *Diamond*

Grill (1996)? Domino's Pizza? No, *Diamond Grill*. About the Chinese café the poet's Canadian-born, Chinese-raised, Scot-Irish-Chinese dad ran in 1950s British Columbia? Diamond stands for good luck in Chinese, Fred Wah's dad says. As a matter of fact, the Diamond Grill brought good luck to the entire Wah family. Fish! Side of fries! Canned vegetables, stick of celery, flowered radishes! Pork sausages, veal chops, little pieces of liver maybe—even I would have learned to cook in Fred Wah's dad's café! But not all was lucky at the Diamond Grill—the racism from the whites for being Chinese, the hassle from the Chinese for being white. Being denied the right to vote until '47 was very unlucky indeed. (The Canadian government repealed the Chinese Exclusion Act not until Canada signed the United Nations Charter of Human Rights after the Second World War, and only because it directly contravened the Charter.) Fred Wah's girlfriend's dad rejected Fred Wah as his daughter's husband ('won't marry no Chinaman'), the silent, simmering anger—. Well, fuck! That was the 1950s—so why you still coming down on your immigrants now? Shae takes yesterday's takeaway box, shoves in the lifeless reeboks like a Domino's pizza and closes the lid. ON THE HOUSE, Shae says, proffering the box to the guests. Meal Deal. Eat! Drink! Be happy! (And why do we always end up in catering?) The guests don't take Shae's 'pizza', they are horrified, they have zero appetite (preferring Chinese). They can't pay us for their room quickly enough. They tip—with regards to the chef. Goodbye, they're off.

Only they aren't (off). They don't make it as far as the door. They don't? They don't. Reeboks? What. Polar bears?! WHAT. Did you see—? No. What about Shae and I?

WE SAW NOTHING WE HEARD EVERYTHING. A synthetic hum (swelling). A very low growl. (Lower. Growler.) Then a thin high pitched thing. Thinning—. Thinning—. Zip! Then silence. The guests—gone. Shae and I turn to each other. In broad daylight, we saw nothing.

Shae has a massive tear in their eye, they tear through the foyer.

IF YOU STILL THINK IT'S A MERITOCRACY GO BACK TO START

The lypard drinks inky ice it devours squid entrails, it has changed colour as a result of its diet maybe. The murky pink carpet with dots (stars) is precisely the kind of night a lypard (this lypard) blends into—*despite* high security lighting. Why stay in the background if you can OWN the foyer. The lypard is OWNING the (our) foyer. Armed with baseball bats and a slingshot (my gold necklace, appropriated), Shae and I are staffing reception. Shae is wearing the *PECS*BET t-shirt with protective padding and boxing headgear (from Sports Direct). I'm wearing triple layers, top and bottom. Cap in lieu of a helmet. I can't see it, I say. Shae, can you? (A synthetic hum.) I can hear it—. There it is, its awful fangs! Where?! There! Gone. We can't leave it, Shae says. We have to do something. Do what? I ask. Deal with it, Shae replies. DEAL WITH IT?! HOW? This is not a series on Netflix, we are not trained military personnel! Doesn't stop Shae (the soldier). You know those buckets of grey paint in the basement? Yes? Get them. Ok, I say, I run I return. More, Shae says. I run I return, I run I return. Now, pour the paint over the carpet, Shae says. But—. DO IT. NOW! Ok, I say. (I'm scared of House Mother Normal, the lypard and Shae, in reverse order.) Pour liberally, Shae says. Smear it across the carpet, go on. Use the broom like a paintbrush. Jesus, I say, what a mess. Normal will *kill*—. Look! It's working! Lypard, I SEE you! The lypard is squirming, it does not like the exposure. It retreats into murky pink parts I haven't yet covered. Baseball bat at the ready, Shae watches my back while I paint every square foot of the carpet. Last corner remaining—is the lypard hiding in there? I can't quite see it—. Neither can I. Shae puts down their baseball bat and opens a fresh bucket of paint. (A very low growl.) Stand back, Shae says. They pour the contents of the bucket into the corner—. (Hissing.) (The big baby crying sound that big cats make.) We catch a glimpse of the lypard's murky pink fur in motion, then nothing. Where is it, I ask. Is it—gone? (Gone where?) This won't be the last we'll see of the lypard, Shae predicts, and they're right.

How to explain the state of the foyer to guests (DIY disaster, British tradespeople). Sorry. Fresh paint—ALL OVER THE CARPET.

Shae's parent is still communicating via the lights, still jumping, sporadically, no reason why not. According to Shae, their parent has taken to sending life affirming messages, too. How's that? I ask. Look, Shae says. Sparks ascending—up the Art Deco tower, and up again, from the bottom to the top? Cava Brut, Shae says, Aldi special buy. Or this one, look. Six flashes at regular intervals? Stella Artois, 6 x 440 ml. It's like they're here, Shae says, while simultaneously being away. Turns out, Shae's parent is next level away. The kind of away that looks you in the eye and sees nothing. (Aldi alcohol.) Shae, I say. My own mum has been locked in a vegetative state since the 1980s, I relate!

Shae says that their parent has also been asking for money. Money, the sheep? No, cash money. (Blink twice for twenty, thrice for thirty—.) Shae's parent is expecting a delivery, apparently. They'll need £ to pay for it.

As far as I'm aware, Money (the sheep) lives in the basement rent-free.

There have been new disappearances, Shae says. No, I say. Yes, Shae says. Two since yesterday. Given that the overall numbers of guest are down (the muck), this amounts to a de facto increase of disappearances (100%). What else, I say. Brace yourself, Shae says. The polar bears are gone. Haha, I say. A hoax, surely. No hoax, Shae says. They are gone.

From where we're at (on top of the reception desk), Shae and I are enjoying an uninterrupted vista of the entire foyer. No lypard, just our gaily painted carpet, unique in the Isle of Wight hospitality sector and beyond. (Where is it.) We see nothing we hear—. Oh don't. WE SEE NOTHING WE HEAR—. A synthetic hum (like an Electronic Dream Plant sound). Where *are* you, I say. No reply. The walls, Shae says. What you mean, I ask. What if it lives up the walls. We look up—THE WALLPAPER MATCHES THE ORIGINAL CARPET DESIGN!!!!! We're surrounded by murky pink walls with lighter dots (stars)—the very night sky that swallows a lypard.

Leopards in the wild use their strength to drag heavy carcasses up very tall trees. No reason why our lypard shouldn't exist in a vertical dimension—. A vertical dimension?! Seriously? Is nothing sacred (PARALLEL)?

The Art Deco tower is famed for its high walls and ceiling, and even the distances between the respective flights of stairs are significant. We need paint rollers with extension poles, Shae says. Carpet Warehouse over the road—go! I slip out. I make the purchase (last money), I slip back in. We start painting the walls like a pair possessed. (It doesn't need to be neat—.) What if we find a carcass, I say, painting. Where, in verticality? We won't, Shae says, we'd see it from here. We extend our poles, we paint higher. WE HEAR—. A high pitched thing. Thinning—. I see it. WHERE. THERE>. Shae was right—the lypard has colonised verticality. It's going up the wall like a murky pink lyzard with dots (stars). Final stretch, we reach maximum (ex)tension (the poles). We push the lypard all the way up to the ceiling—it hangs there like a back-up Lee Bul chandelier. Shae and I drop our weapons I mean decorating tools. What now?! The lypard is out of our reach entirely, like almost everything.

When, again, are things going to start looking up for Shae and I? Wasn't Shae going to escape their working-class destiny? (The Reebok Working Class Plus fits, but also doesn't?) Weren't they going to mobilise what cultural capital they have acquired through grafting, and weren't they going to work their way out of their less than dreamy job and situation? Ah. Yes. Yes, they were. But no. Sorry. Sorry, but no. (Double twist.) Shae isn't going to work their way out of anything, and it's not for a lack of trying—.

This is Portland, Oregon, the 1990s. The US of

A. Tonya Harding is a working-class figure skater. She's got talent, she throws everything at it. She's the first female skater to attempt and land a triple axel in competition (the technically most difficult jump in her discipline). Skating ten times better than her competitors, Harding gets half the score—losing points for her 'unpalatable', 'unrefined', or 'unfeminine'aesthetic'. (This is what class means.) To the regret of USFS officials (the national governing body for the sports in the US), Tonya Harding qualifies for the '94 Lillehammer Winter Olympics. (This is not the kind of femininity that America wants to present to the world.) In the months leading up to the games, Harding's ex-husband Jeff Gillooly orchestrates an attack on fellow Olympian Nancy Kerrigan. (Gillooly's collaborator strikes Keegan's knee with a telescopic baton.) Gillooly serves time in prison for the attack, and his name becomes synonymous with the act of kneecapping: to gillooly someone (gilloolied, gilloolying). Harding herself is charged, but avoids a prison sentence by pleading guilty for some minor offenses including hindering the prosecution. As part of the bargain, she is banned from the US Figure Skating Association for life. Age 23, Tonya Harding's career is over. Her background caught up with her, put her right back in her place. Her talent and grafting did nothing to save her—this is what class means. Harding's skates are just Reeboks with blades on.

Killing the classic triumph over tragedy narrative expertly—but the lypard? We cannot get rid. At this juncture, Shae and I are forced to shut shop. We are closing the New House of Normal for business like the bailiffs closed Ryde Arena in October '17.

EMPIRE 2.0

The Isle of Wight's Needles Headland is an area of outstanding natural beauty (rock formations, cliff drops). With its concrete walkways curving along the top of the cliff, ramps and the remnants of two giant gantries (rocket launching stations), it is also a major site of the now defunct British space programme (early '50s until '71). The soldier (Shae) and I are here for good reason—they built starships here once. We require a starship to whisk us away. (Nothing but a starship will do.) (A rocket to the moon will do.) Public perception is that the UK never even had a space programme it was so low key ('top secret'), but it did, it did! One way tkts to the moon, please, thank you, I say, or preferably to some other planet that isn't a US colony. Five £, the National Trust volunteer in the ticket booth says. The tkts will grant you entry to the onsite bunker (former research facilities). The onsite bunker? I say. Is that it?! What about take off? What a come down—! Shae looks at me, have you lost it.

When we get back to the hotel, the foyer is packed. What's happening?! This isn't safe! We are closed due to serious concerns for public health and wellbeing (the lypard). Violet Club is a party, apparently. (An illegal party.) One of the party goers, Yellow Sun, says they are British which tells you they are lying (no sun). Brown Bunny, the elderly poet, writes absolute fireworks on their phone, Green Bamboo (who?) is hopping mad (at Brown Bunny). I go looking for the reeboks—there they are, I can barely get through to them. Can you explain what's going on, I say. Violet Club, the reeboks say (party). Party, I say. Yes, party. Green Grass—Green *Bamboo*, I thought. No, Green Grass, too. They are different—ok, Green Grass *what*. Nothing, forget it. The reeboks are moving on, and so is the conversation. Party goer Blue Streak crisis manages an ongoing spat, Purple Possum is on track to ruining everyone's evening. Shae, I say, who are they? Are they local? Online acquaintances of the reeboks, Shae replies. Grindr? Not Grindr. Yellow Sun works in fashion, apparently, the hashtags sunboy and artificallightbois appealed. Blue Streak caught glimpses of our Art Deco foyer on the photo of Shae and I, modelling, which led them to conceive of Violet Club (party). Yellow Sun and

Blue Streak kept DMing Shae and me, apparently, no reply (too busy). They tracked down the reeboks (via #NewHouseofNormal) who were susceptible to the idea (party) on the grounds of their own relative isolation. Ok, I say, fair. But Violet Club, Yellow Sun, Brown Bunny, Green Bamboo, Green Grass, Blue Streak? What else, Purple Possum? Violet, yellow, brown, green, green again, blue and purple?! Really?

Accredited to San Franciscan Gilbert Baker (gay hero), the 1978 design of the rainbow flag comprised hot pink, red, orange, yellow, green, turquoise, indigo, violet. Not violet, yellow, brown, green, green again, blue and purple? No—. Was Gilbert Baker a military man. Yes. Why u asking. Just asking—.

While the most recent work on rocketry conducted at the Needles site revolved around civic satellite launchers (for example, a project called Black Knight in the 1960s), all of it—ALL OF IT— goes back to the military, and most of it to nuclear weaponry. Black Knight came out of Blue Streak, a ballistic missile capable of carrying a megaton range nuclear warhead to strategically important parts of the Soviet Union.

Violet Club is not a giant party. Brown Bunny is not a party animal, and Purple Possum is not the life and soul—they're just not. The rainbow codes were a series of randomly selected combinations of colours and nouns from a list (wt list), meant to disguise the nature of various British military research projects between the Second World War and the late 1950s.

Violet Club was a nuclear weapon deployed by the United Kingdom during the Cold War. Green Bamboo was a one megaton thermonuclear warhead, Yellow Sun was the first British operational high-yield strategic nuclear weapon (outer casing only). Green Grass, also known as the Interim Megaton Weapon, was its, Yellow Sun's, nuclear warhead. Purple Possum was a nerve agent. Brown Bunny (which later became Blue Bunny) was the project to store nuclear mines on the continent, to be detonated by wire in the event of a Soviet invasion. Brown Bunny was not only designed to destroy facilities and installations over a large area, but also to deny occupation of the area to an enemy for an appreciable time due to contamination.

Let's go, Shae says, let's get out of here. Go where? I ask. Nature, Shae replies. When, now? Yes. Now.

Following the USA and the Soviet Union, the UK was the third state to develop a thermonuclear weapon in 1954 (a very large pure fission bomb with a yield of one megaton). A Cold War participant that nobody cared about, pursuing the dream of a vertical empire—.

What if the rainbow codes inspired the design of

the original rainbow flag. No. Don't even go there—
the rainbow codes were a British thing and unlikely
to have inspired Gilbert Baker from Kansas, USA!
But he was in the military once—. Yes. Dismissed on
the grounds of 'effeminacy'.

The most recent attempt at a progressive design
introduces white, pink, light blue, brown and black
stripes in the shape of an arrow in the left half of the
flag, while retaining the iconic rainbow on the right.
The light blue, pink and white stripes on the left
come from the transgender flag, originally designed
by Monica Helm in '99. The brown and black
stripes are meant to foreground LGBTQI+ people
of colour, as well as those living with AIDS and the
dead. I like it, I say. Down with all flags, Shae says.

At night, the Needles rocket testing site is
tremendous full-stop. Cliff drops, concrete walkways,
barbed wire, moonlight and the sea. British nature
is so interconnected with military and empire,
I say. No beach without Sellafield. No garden
without Dungeness. (Sellafield was the world's
first nuclear power station to deliver electricity in
commercial quantities, but its original purpose was
the production of weapons-grade plutonium.) My
own sense of beauty is brutal, I am already British
like that. On Shae, the scenery is currently lost. They
have urgent business to attend to, like scaling what's

left of the (left) gantry, its concrete foundations. They climb really high, they are high above sea level now. Shae is tying our flag to the mast (the t-shirt with the pink-mouthed shark and the black and white stripy flashes). Look—! OUR FLAG IS FLYING AT THE HIGHEST POINT OF THE ISLAND! WHAMBAM! it says on said t-shirt which will be seen by a National Trust volunteer in the morning. WHAMBAM! Good morning—. Hah! Hah!

It isn't just British nature which is imperial. Everything is (the Needles, the British space rocket programme, the Solent and its forts). Sandown Zoo is (located inside a Victorian military fort). The rainbow flag? (Shhh—.) We don't like to talk about it (we are British). But Britishness itself is mediated through empire which is why colonial nostalgia can be recruited into neo-imperial agendas (like Tory Brexit, or 'Empire 2.0') like *that*.

Take 'Independence Day', just an example and a rhetoric peddled in the final stages of the Brexit campaign. Traditionally, any 'Independence Day' marks the liberation of an ex-colony from imperial power—independence *from* Britain, perhaps. Associating voluntary EU membership with colonial rule, while at the same time harking back to a past where 'we' (Britain) 'either conquered or invaded 178 nations of the world' (Boris Johnson in his 2016 Conservative party conference speech, to cheers from the hall), is messy metaphorical twisting (dangerous and offensive)—but for those with a Brexit agenda, it worked: 'we' voted to leave. Imperial rhetoric tends to 'work'—such is empire's stranglehold on the British psyche and reality.

All work on rocketry on the Isle of Wight effectively stopped in '71. Ironically, the systems that were built and tested in the '60s, and then abandoned, could have been highly commercially successful in the '80s and '90s (communication satellites, weather observation). This was perfectly predictable at the time—.

Since 2010, the UK Space Agency in Surrey is responsible for the British civil space programme (coordinating UK efforts in fields such as earth science, telecoms and space exploration). We (the UK) are currently *not speaking* to the European Space Agency—they have threatened to exclude us from Galileo (the project to devise a European satellite navigation system), post-Brexit. (Spiteful Europeans.) We (the UK) have publicly vowed to launch our own independent British satellite system instead. Rocketry may yet become the next booming sector in the UK—other than, say, the hotel industry. SO, WILL THERE BE JOBS FOR STELLAR MECHANICS? Shae asks. Shae—! I say.

I can't believe they just said that.

This is Ryde High Street, the Wimpy kids are vaping outside Barclays. They got, of all things, Ralphie on a leash. You seen yr boss lately? a Wimpy kid asks. No, Shae replies. House Mother Normal took off owing the Wimpy kids £, apparently. They'll be holding Ralphie hostage until his owner returns and coughs up. Nice to catch up on the little things, Shae says.

A group of twenty-somethings walk by with their Staffies (called Karate, or Judo). They look just like Justin Bieber, but paler. Fags, the Wimpy kids shout. You got AIDS! They make obscene (gay) gestures, employing their mouths primarily. Wasters, the twenty-somethings retort. Shouldn't you be at school? They stop. Judo wriggles over to Ralphie. (Judo, sit!) Why don't you do something useful with your time, Justin Bieber says to the Wimpy kids. Look—. He is trying to hand Wimpy leader a Tory leaflet (*Forward, Together*), a UKIP badge (*Britain Together*). Sssssss! Wimpy leader hisses, pulling away. No way! See my t-shirt?! Wimpy leader pulls on her PACCBET t-shirt in an intimidating way, stepping forward (posturing). Manufactured by migrant workers—*her* (me). And see this one (Wimpy k smoking a vape)? Polish. Czech, whatever. Got it?!

In silent agreement, the Wimpy kids close rank

behind their leader. They subtly arm themselves (empty Stella bottles, full Vimto cans). Under their breath, they cuss (tory fags, faggy toffs). So, Wimpy leader says, breaking the neck off of a bottle. You were saying? (Barking.) (That's the dogs going berserk.) Ok ok—the twenty-somethings don't want the hassle nor the muck on their clothes, they back off. Your loss, they say. Cmon (to Karate, to Judo). GO HOME (to Shae and I). (Home—.) Freakoes (to Shae and I). For now, they split. They know how to bide their time, they are strategic.

Justin Biebers—I recognise them as the demonstrators on Ryde beach earlier this year. They used to be UKIP or EDL (LGBTQI+ divisions), but they're Tory now. Better career options—they might go into politics professionally. They blame immigration for sky-high unemployment rates on the island. Unlike the Wimpy kids, they don't get into fisticuffs. They might recruit intimidation tactics, like placing a defaced sheep outside a hotel with migrant employees (no real harm there). They, occasionally, might tip off Immigration. They've seen Shae and I around and they WANT. US. OUT. They think that, by association, our queerness brings their gayness into disrepute. (Great.) (Really great.) (How many times can you divide a minority culture—.) (How many times can you divide the Isle of Wight?)

Ralphie the Labrador is looking a little overwhelmed. He suddenly bolts—.

UPSIDE DOWN

Fully armed (baseball bats, slingshot), Shae and I are in the foyer. We're dressed for the grande finale— Shae is wearing their *PECS*BET big cat handling gear including boxing helmet, I'm wearing my pastel pink dress with the white collar and knee-high socks. There's a bucket of squid intestines and icy ink in front of the reception desk. Present yourself, Shae says, rattling the bucket. No avail—the lypard prefers to stick to its upside down territory (it clings to the ceiling). I bait it, I smack my lips. Nothing. Is this what you want?! Shae says. They get up on the reception desk and start slinging shots in the lypard's direction. Whack! (Missile hits ceiling.) Come down—. Whack! IT PHWAR! FALLS FROM THE CEILING WHERE IT LIVES AND ONTO THE RECEPTION DESK. It roars, it is LIVID. Shae drops their slingshot, they lunge for the baseball bat. The lypard lashes out, Shae falls backwards. Shae's had it, I think, but they haven't, had it. The lypard isn't coming for Shae. It's coming for me. It hits me with its terrible paw—. A light comes on, top landing. (NOT NOW.) Another light comes on, entrance level, left corner. (NOT. NOW.) (Shae's parent? Can it wait?!) Next light, first flight of stairs—strobing. (Is this Berghain?) Second flight of stairs (on), then third—an upwards trend. Why am I even in a position to witness this? The lypard is transfixed by the lights—is Shae's parent a lypard tamer? WHAM! The lypard is hit. GET. OFF. HER, Shae says, reloading their slingshot. BAM! The lypard yelps. It is all too much for the big cat (the light show, the being shot at), it decides to remove itself. It grabs and drags me into its upside down territory—.

Shae? No Shae. I'm up here alone. I hear the lypard in the distance. (Humming, a v low hum.) Lights, sparkly lights above, or is that below. Movement nearby. Oh wow—it's Ramayya's incredible lions, they have been known to hunt and kill lypards, or to disarm them under their vomit hearts! The lions stand up on their hind legs, they are facing each other. Their insignificant genitalia are covered with flowers. They kiss with lizard tongues, and the atmosphere is positively electric.

I decide to go for a walk. I hear a roar—more big cats? No. Applause. It's Tonya Harding, having a moment—not in an ice rink, but in a boxing arena. (Girl reinvents herself in middle-age, I'm just stating the facts.) Heavyweight champion of the upside down world! TON-YA, TON-YA! The audience loves boxing Harding. Oh good. Good to see. Preferable to the mauled body and jersey sweater I expected to find. Outside of her figure skating career, Tonya Harding comes to the attention of the media on the following occasions: in '94, she uses mouth-to-mouth resuscitation to help revive a pensioner who collapsed in a bar in Portland, Oregon. In '95, Harding's band, the Golden Blades, are booed off stage at their only ever performance, also in Portland. In '03, Harding makes her professional boxing debut, losing in a four round decision in the undercard of the Mike Tyson Clifford Etienne fight. Like Tonya Harding, I'm moving on. No point dwelling on things.

Is it getting hot up here? Here is young Shae. Shae (21) looks like a Goldsmiths student. They're wearing their dark herringbone woollen overcoat from Oxfam over their paint stained white t-shirt. Black ankle duster chinos, white sports socks and black DMs. Crop hair cut combed forward, dyed yellow. This student, Shae Benet (21), is enrolled at this university (this is different dimension type stuff). It's not like Shae (16) left school with two GCSEs (it's not like they started grafting too late). It's not like they (17) never took A-levels. It's not like they couldn't enrol on a degree as a result, and it's not like they (21) are self-educating like the world's leading unenrolled student towards absolutely no academic qualification. In this alternate reality, Shae Benet (21) is about to graduate from their Fine Art or English Literature or Media and Cultural Studies degree with a 2.1. Not sorted, exactly, in terms of their future, but they're in with a fighting chance.

What's happening, are these thunderclouds. I spot the lypard—it's over there, where once were Nisha Ramayya's magical lions. It's snacking on flowers, they are its salad. (What did it do to the lions?!) I steer clear and into a different scenario. Oh hi! It's Shae's parent. You got the invitation? Shae's parent asks. (The lights.) I did, as it were. Let's bake together, Shae's parent says. (Ok, Shae's *mum*.) Shae's mum hands me a child-size rolling pin, a star-shaped biscuit cutter and a small plastic bowl containing eggs, flour, sugar and baking powder. Kneading, I copy Shae's mum's every move. I'm allowed to eat dough from the bowl (salmonella are probiotics in this dimension). Kittenish, the lypard walks into the kitchen. Jesus Christ, it is gagging for a dessert! Shae's mum feeds it some biscuits, she drinks from a glass on the edge of the work surface (repeatedly).

You got something for me? Shae's mum gets to the point. Maybe, I say, pulling a sachet of barbiturates out of my sleeve. Can you pay? I ask. ('Take the £ upfront.') Shae's mum isn't impressed (coming here, eating my food, demanding money for a small return favour—). Shae will give you the £ later, she says. (Two blinks for twenty, three for thirty—.) Ok, I say (that's not upfront). We trade, a sachet of barbies (expertly laced by House Mother Normal) for thirty quid (to be paid by Shae on my return). Don't mix wt acohol, I caution on my way out. Shae's mum gives me the V sign (her blessing), she's not currently interested in me.

I move towards a purple part of the upside down. (I thought purple was good but no, purple is toxic.) There's House Mother Normal reunited with her dog, Ralphie. You got something for me? House Mother Normal asks. She wants £. Not yet, I reply, nervously. UOME, House Mother Normal says. Lying at his owner's feet, Ralphie is looking a little worse for wear, I must say. That dog is always licking things, no wonder he's got a case of the salmonella (the non-probiotic, sick-making kind). Honestly? He looks lifeless. Like he's on his way out. Why prolong a dying dog's misery? I can help, I say, I can end it like *that*. I can clasp Ralphie's doggy heart without lifting a finger, crush it telekinetically, if it's the ethical thing to do—. (In return for the service, you write off my debt?)

The CIA and the US military have conducted largely illegal research into military applications of psychic abilities since the First World War at least. For example, the Stargate Project (aka 'Grill Flame') famously and unsuccessfully trained subjects to kill test animals by willing their (the test animals') hearts to slow down, then stop. These histories have inspired the *Stranger Things* series on Netflix, especially the child character Eleven. Eleven, like Blue Streak, is a Cold War technology. Eleven can access other dimensions—the Soviet Union, that most alternate of dimensions according to some—primarily for the purpose of international espionage. She has psychokinetic abilities for the purpose of inflicting bodily harm on communist others. I'm not Eleven, of course, I'm 36. I don't will Ralphie's heart to slow down, I don't will it to stop. Actually, Ralphie is looking much better already. I don't think my talents are needed here. Time to return to normality—but what fresh h i t?!

On an upside down world type reception desk lies a letter informing me that my application for British citizenship has been accepted. (Wt? Did my application submit itself? Did the alternate Home Office accept my Mickey Mouse residence card?

Yes of course they did—they issued it in the first place!) (A pro-immigration governmental body sets this Home Office's very different agenda.) *You are required to take part in a British citizenship ceremony*, the letter informs me. *Please book an appointment with your alternate registration service within three weeks of receiving this letter.* I call a landline—. (Am I hearing a phone ringing nearby?) I get through to the alternate registration service straight away. Their IT booking system is fool proof and highly reliably, it has never knowingly crashed or been down for any significant periods of time. Appointment sorted!

There's Shae (36), wearing a two tone two piece. They're with House Mother Normal who's in full drag. They're both holding union jack paper flags. (A citizenship ceremony hosted by the New House of Normal? Ok, I've seen stranger things—.) Before we begin—, Shae the registrar says. There's an issue with me wearing plimsolls, apparently. (No jeans no trainers policy.) Really? But Shae is wearing Reeboks with their two piece! And House Mother Normal's dress and fishnets are effectively ripped, her crown skewiff—anyway, I comply, I take off my plimsolls. I consent to being naturalised in socks, now do I satisfy the regulations. Shae hands me a union jack paper flag. (Wave it.) (I wave it.) Repeat after me, Shae instructs. *I (name).* I (name), I say.

Do solemnly, sincerely and truly declare and affirm. Do solemnly, sincerely and truly declare and affirm. *That on becoming a British Citizen.* That on becoming a British Citizen. *I will be faithful and bear true allegiance to her Majesty Queen Mother Normal the First, her heirs and successors, according to the law.* I hesitate. Say it, Shae says. I will be faithful and bear true allegiance to her Majesty Queen Mother Normal the First, her heirs and successors, according to the law, I say. You are now British, Shae declares. Hip hip—hurray! Hip hip—hurray! Hip hip—hurray! We shake hands, my religion does not prevent me from doing so. Here's your Mickey Mouse citizenship certificate, hold it up. (*Your certificate must not be unofficially altered or laminated.*) Before you go—, Shae says. They take an official photograph of me, my certificate, the flag and the queen, Her Majesty Queen Mother Normal the First. They take £160 off me for the ceremony (in this respect, this alternate authority is no different to, say, the Isle of Wight Council, or Southwark Council). £14 for a JPEG of the photo. A cup of tea, however, is free. Again, I'm just stating the facts.

I pass through a mustard-shaped, warmer part of the upside down, I'm glad I'm wearing my airy pink dress. This is the part where working-class people including working-class migrants live in quality social housing in Central London. (Stop it.) (Is this dimension selling me BS, I increasingly think so. Social housing in London? Micky Mouse citizenships, Queen Mother Normal the First? WORKING-CLASS GRADUATES?) (This is Tory Britain, repeat after me.) Baking mums, boxing ice skaters and lions with insignificant genitalia—nice remembering the possibility of you. Now, where did that purple go. (Where's reality, I want to change it.) Ah, over there, I return to toxicity—and here is your proof. If ever there were any doubt, here is your proof that the upside down, too, is a shitshow. Under a venomous cloud the lypard sits. It sits on a pile of polar bear meat and everything that is good. High pitched electric crackling, ochre thunder. A beige and yellow checkered lightning bolt strikes from above, or is that below. It travels across the height, width and depth of Tory reality including my body. Violence wz here, it says in the lypard's eyes. Violence wz here all along.

Like the lypard, I navigate dimensions. I move between different dimensions like a figure skater might move between poses, or between careers.

I'm back in the foyer, mid-action. Shae's FACE when they see me (aw). They are firing slingshot pellets against the ceiling, the lypard falls from it (hot on my heels). This time, it'll have me. It looks so determined. Run, Shae says. RUUUUUUUN!!!

I RUN OUT OF THE FOYER AND DOWN THE STAIRS I RUN ALONG A CORRIDOR LEADING INTO THE BASEMENT. I HEAR THE LYPARD BEHIND ME I TEAR OPEN THE DOOR TO THE BASEMENT. Then I stop. I just—stop. I turn I wait. The lypard has a massive tear in its eye it tears down the corridor towards me. I lower my head. Lypard lypard—your eyes are tearing. Are you diamond? Probably not! *We*'re made of diamond stuff, that is, harder stuff than you're made of—. I tear Ramayya's vomit heart from its sky I use it like a deadly lasso. I rope the lypard I tighten the lasso around its neck I—WHOAAAAAA!—throw it over my head and into the basement! (It flies like a robin or a hand grenade—.) I flick my chin to the right (ANGER), the basement door slams shut behind me. Then, silence. Just me, I radiate psychic energy.

ECZEMA! on the back of my legs, ECZEMA! down the lengths of my arms. My torso is WET, it is WEEPING! I'm sorry I'm flaring up—.

Maria Fusco the writer wrote in bold letters with exclamation mark—ECZEMA!—what I barely touched upon. Had I been asked to talk eczema, pre-Fusco, I'd have put my index fingers into the shape of a cross (exorcise now—). (Exercise doesn't help. It makes eczema worse, but seawater, apparently, with its antiseptic properties works wonders on the affected skin.) Now Fusco's performance piece is doing the talking (ECZEMA!), and I imagine it's talking shamelessly—Fusco is good on the body.

Shae? I say, to no one. The lypard—I think I got it.

I THOUGHT THE SEA WAS THE GAYEST THING ON THE ISLAND BUT NO

I look like Eleven from *Stranger Things*, I'm 36. Similar hair, similar face. Similar fears (childhood terrors). Fears rhymes with fierce, this is no coincidence, not in this house. *The Tyger* by William Blake (1794) is one of four canonical poems included in the Life in the UK test official handbook. Romantic verse is not normally part of Shae nor my educational capital but there you go—a lypard is a literary leopard (to a naturalised British citizen).

We are on the rooftop (above the upside down), looking at stars. In London, I never saw a star (light pollution). Have a Milky Way. Go on. Or a Galaxy—. Mars bar? I go for the Milky Way, thanks.

In Mojisola Adebayo's play *Stars* (2018), the characters share a Milky Way and a vape in a Peckham council flat. They talk about Lieutenant Uhura from *Star Trek* and Mae Jemison, the first black woman in space. The Dogon of Mali, Adebayo writes, had infinitely superior knowledge of the solar system, compared to pre-Renaissance Western astronomers. These West African ancients already knew about Jupiter's moons, Saturn's rings and Sirius A's white dwarf companion Sirius B. They knew that the earth revolved around the sun. (How.) (They had superior analytical skills, or a hotline to well-informed spirits.) (How—is that surprising.)

Another 'surprise': fantasies of Empire 2.0 are met with ZERO ENTHUSIASM by Britain's former colonies. 'We' might be pushing for non-EU trade deals rn, but the Commonwealth nations are largely disinclined to become Britain's post-Brexit dogsbodies. (Kinder Surprise—.)

Imagine doing (voting for) something (Brexit), that will affect you detrimentally—FOR A LAUGH. (Paul Willis again.) Counter establishment cultures run deep through working-class Britain, they travel down generations.

'We' have thrown Shae and I under the bus. Ahahahaha—! Happy to.

The letter from the actual UK Home Office arrives the next day, several months after I first applied for permanent residence. My application is refused on the grounds of, what, failure to provide sufficient evidence of any of the following 'qualified activities': 1) Employment. 2) Self-employment. 3) Unemployment. 4) Study, with private health insurance. 5) Economic self-sufficiency. Specifically, I failed to prove 1) Employment. Why? No pay slips. (I know.) No letters from past or present employers. (YES I KNOW.) National Insurance contributions? (Leave me alone—.) I have worked in the UK for twenty years—UNDER THE TAX THRESHOLD. For twenty years, I have consistently earned less than the annual tax allowance (£11850 rn) which renders me illegible in terms of immigration law. When I first took up the job at the New House of Normal in March, I requested a letter confirming employment. House Mother Normal just looked at me. (Are you joking.) As far as the tax office goes, my boss doesn't know me.

What's tht bollocks box of chocolates talk—life is like the Pass the Parcel game in B. S. Johnson's *House Mother Normal*, more like. (No Mars bar Galaxy Milky Way inside the parcel, only dog shit.) (That will teach them not to expect anything from life.) (Important life lesson.) (Cruel to be kind, that sort of thing.) Present-day House Mother Normal will be terrorising the upside down territory for the foreseeable future, so Shae and I have reopened shop in her absence. We'll run this place on a cash only basis until they'll evict us, deport us, or drive us out, or until hotel guests will start contracting Legionnaires disease (ancient pipes). Whatever will happen—we will adapt. For all intents and purposes, we *are* Tonya Harding.

What if fear, rage, joy and a sense of humour were actually Milky Ways. What if political urgency, transgression and difference were Kinder Surprises! What if WE THINK YOU ARE BORING were a funsize Mars bar. What if life (a lot of it) and love (above all) were mini Galaxies, then there'd be Celebrations for Shae and I after all! Shame the moment can't be had under a starry sky, it's literally starting to drizzle right now.

The lypard is yapping at night (like a baby), disturbing the guests and getting on everyone's nerves.

Rain is whipping down. The sea is ferocious. What looks like a 1930s brutalist building—a circular concrete structure—is actually a Victorian military fort right by the seafront. (Are we back where we started? Storming invincible forts? No—.) Inside *this* fort, is Sandown Zoo. Like all things Sandown, the zoo is derelict. On top of the building, a mid-century concrete sculpture of—of all things—a leopard strides majestically towards the sea. (Queen.) (A red white orange black power stride, set in concrete.) Look, I say, looking up. Ferocious thing, Shae says. Shae has got the lypard on a leash (that's *the* lypard, *our* lypard). We brought it here, to break it gently. Watch, Shae says to the lypard. Watch closely—.

English Channel throws an opening salve at Sandown leopard—roooOOAARRR (that's the sea, the English Channel). Sandown leopard retaliates, flashing its fangs, blinging its red and orange. Heh English flannel! You scared already? English Channel responds with a gurgle (a cruel laugh). It launches a deep swell, driving a breaker towards Sandown leopard. WHOAAA!! (Shae, the lypard and I sustain the force of it.) (Bit blustery out. Bit wet.) Sandown leopard, if anything, looks fiercer when wet. Thing is sparkling, ok! (Sandown leopard is the gayest thing on the Isle of Wight—I thought the sea was, but no.) English Channel retreats (temporarily). We wait. It's pouring with rain. We hear a low growl. Lower. Growler. English Channel releases a rogue wave. (Rogue waves impact with tremendous force, breaking at a hundred tons per square metre—we break more easily.) HERE IT COMES!!★!★!!!!!!★!★! Wave breaks, we don't. As the water recedes, Sandown leopard is positively gloating. Is that it, EC? You spent? And, believe it or not, here it stops. Sandown lypard defeats English Channel with its facial expressions only.

Incredibly, the lypard, *our* lypard, makes like a puppy before the Sandown leopard. It's actually grovelling. Nothing like a day by the sea to put you in touch with your own relative insignificance, Shae says.

Once, in the 1970s, The Times newspaper labelled the Isle of Wight Zoo 'the slum zoo of Britain'. I'd steer clear of that kind of language, but judging from the state of the building alone, I don't think we're that far from the '70s situation now. A 'slum zoo' in Sandown and a nation in decline, but here we go. What a life.

'Overpriced and the worlds smallest zoo I've ever been to, if that's what you can even call it. We walked round the whole thing in 35 minutes are you having us on.'

'I feel robbed of my money ! This zoo & let's face it they've more neck than a giraffe to call it that ! But honestly it's the worst zoo I've ever been to in my whole life ! All the animals looked like they'd been drugged with some powerful sedative & that was all of 5 that we actually managed to see. Literally walked round it in less than an hour, & 10 mins of that was for a fag break , very disappointing.'

'The children was board and we was done sooner then what I thought we was going to be.'

'when we got back to hectors cage there they were again wild rats ,I think you have got a vermin problem ,'

'Queued for 25 mins while ticketing staff battled with computer ticket system . 2 staff on duty both unable to work systems , when I made the point about how inefficient their system was they gave me death stare ! Having to ask for the key to access the ice cream display and then wait with melting ice creams as staff try to deal with ice cream orders was the limit . The plus was the Tiger sightings except for the very sick one poor thing show classic stress pattern weaving .'

'unless we missed something there are not many animals. they have a huge meerkat enclosure with three meerkats in it, they were hiding until the keeper went in to flush them out. The Lion & Tigers were all hiding.'

'The meerkats were nowhere to be seen except for one lonely meerkat walking around.'

'I understand that they have suffered a loss of lots of their animals however this doesn't excuse the absence of animals, literally, we have been and gone and seen everything within 25 minutes, two lions and two tigers doesn't make a zoo, apparently there are five tigers being rescued from a circus in Spain arriving soon, maybe they will need rescuing from here soon.'

'all they market their Zoo on is the white tiger and then he's not there'

'Wuld rather set fire to the money then spend it to go in here .'

'The highlight was when the lion was offered a treat. It was a cardboard box filled with straw and dog poo.'

'Fun time's at the zoo! It even has a tiny museum about it's past life during World War 2 and Operation Pluto.'

'First impressions suggest the zoo has seen better days, but then, it is situated in a historical fort that was also utilised during WW2! The zoo has a mini exhibition of P.L.U.T.O (Pipe Line Underwater Transportation of Oil), which was a project to construct pipelines under the English Channel between England and France in support of the Allied invasion of Normandy in 44!!'

'The place culd do with a few quids thrown at it to bring it back to its hole glory.'

'On arrival I thought it was derelict. It looked like it probably closed 30 years ago. It stands next to a crumbling hotel or casino. It was raining and there were few cars in the car park. The first thing you see is a statue of a large cat on top of the zoo walls. The run down look of the building continued inside. We had to walk through mud and huge puddles to reach the animal enclosures.'

'Isle of Wight Zoo is only really suitable for a dry day.'

'Attended on a rainy day.'

'Great day out even thou it was purring with rain.'

'I was really excited to see the tiger and the jaguar but to be honest they both looked even more depressed than I felt.'

'I just felt uneasy about this zoo, the enclosures were too small especially the jaguars enclosure and I felt uncomfortable at his constant pacing. I don't understand how it is deemed acceptable to allow such animals to have an environment so inadequate.'

'Visited the zoo today, omg its the worst zoo ever, all the enclosures need clearing out and tidying up, also enclosures are rather small especially for big cats, iv never seen a lion looking so depressed, he was laying in cage that was tiny, and the expression on his face was so upsetting, he wasn't really moving I actually thought he was a stuffed toy until he turned his head then flopped onto his side, saw a couple who had paid to feed the jaguar and get it to do tricks like it was circus animal and the zoo want £140 to do it. There was a little monkey who had previously been attacked and bitten by a bigger monkey and not been separated to heal and we watched it get hit by the big monkey then the big monkey kept poking the bleeding wound then licking his fingers.'

'Its nice to see theyve put new buildings and educational things but sorting out the enclosures would have been better. Your see what i mean in the pictures.'

'The worst part about it was the keepers had the nerve to say that the animals weren't stressed while pacing and were quite happy in the surroundings. THEY CLEARLY WERE NOT and anyone that knows the animals well can tell they are stressed and not happy. And as for the Lemurs they were nowhere to be seen. the only thing we saw was through a dirty window into a dirty inside part of the cage was 2 curled up so carefully not to come into contact with the tons of poo that was everywhere.'

'Half an hour of my life I can't get back.'

'This is a con.'

'Symptomatic.'

'The staff really do try.'

'Desolate.'

'Heartbreaking.'

REFERENCES

Adebayo, Mojisola (2018) 'Stars'. In Waidner, Isabel (ed.) *Liberating the Canon: An Anthology of Innovative Literature*. Manchester: Dostoyevsky Wannabe.

Bernard, Jay (2016) *The Red and Yellow Nothing*. London: Ink Sweat & Tears Press.

Cooper, Dennis (2017) 'Astro Float Materials Present... How to Build a Parade Float', 10 July 2017, *DC's: The blog of author Dennis Cooper*. https://denniscooperblog.com/astro-float-materials-presents-how-to-build-a-parade-float-2/

Delany, Samuel (1969/2008) 'The Star Pit'. In *Aye, and Gomorrah, and Other Stories*. London: Vintage Edition.

Department of the Army (2014) Pamphlet 70-3: Army Acquisition Procedures. http://www.acqnotes.com/Attachments/Army%20Pamplet%2070-3%20Acquisitions.pdf

Fusco, Maria (2018) *ECZEMA!* Performance piece. National Theatre Wales, 28 July 2018.

Hill, CN (2001) *A Vertical Empire: The History of the UK Rocket and Space Programme, 1950-1971.* London: Imperial College Books.

The Home Office (2017) *Life in the United Kingdom: A Guide for New Residents (3rd Edition).* London: Stationary Office.

I, Tonya (2017). [Film] Directed by Craig Gillespie. United States: LuckyChap Entertainment.

Johnson, B. S. (1971/2004) 'House Mother Normal: A Geriatric Comedy'. In *Omnibus.* London: Picador.

Puar, Jasbir K. (2006) *Terrorist Assemblages: Homonationalism in Queer Times.* Durham and London: Duke University Press.

Pico, Tommy (2017) *Nature Poem.* Portland: Tin House Books.

Ramayya, Nisha (2018) Poem read at Oxford, Queen's College, 11 May 2018 (as part of 'An Aspirin the Size of the Sun', organised by Grace Linden and Ogazielum Mba).

Sarkar, Ash (2018) 'The past really is another

country. Let's leave Boris Johnson there', 10 July 2018, *The Guardian*. https://www.theguardian.com/commentisfree/2018/jul/10/past-boris-johnson-colonial-brexit-colony

Scottee (2018) 'IT GETS WORSE'. *Unwanted Collaborations*. Acrylic paint on canvas.

Stranger Things (2016). [TV series] Directed by The Duffer Brothers. United States: Netflix.

Trip Advisor (2018) Reviews: The Isle of Wight Zoo, https://www.tripadvisor.co.uk/Attraction_Review-g191249-d263366-Reviews-Isle_of_Wight_Zoo-Sandown_Isle_of_Wight_England.html

Wah, Fred (1996/2006) *Diamond Grill*. Alberta: NeWest Press.

Willis, Paul (1977/2000) *Learning to Labour: How Working Class Kids Get Working Class Jobs*. Farnham: Ashgate.

THANKS

Victoria Brown and Richard Brammer,
Dostoyevsky Wannabe.

Richard Porter, for Queers Read This.

Linda Stupart, for the artwork.

Early readers: Dodie Bellamy, Lisa Blackman, Anna
Glendenning, Nisha Ramayya, Joanna Walsh.

Lisa Blackman, for everything and the island.

★

Support non-Oxbridge talent.

★

Printed in Great
Britain
by Amazon